TIME UNDER TENSION

A KELSEY JAMES FITNESS MYSTERY:
BOOK ONE

KRISTINA FOX

Book Cover by Getcovers.com

First edition 2025

ISBN: 979-8-89694-104-0 - eBook

ISBN: 979-8-89694-105-7 - Paperback

ISBN: 979-8-89694-106-4 - Hardcover

To my three little bears, who taught me the true meaning of resilience and have always inspired me to be the best version of myself.

CONTENTS

Chapter 1

Saturday, September 10, 2022

The morning sun poured through the bay window of Fox Fitness, casting a warm glow across the gym floor. The enticing aroma of freshly brewed coffee wafted in from Blake's Coffee Shop next door and mingled with the fresh morning air.

"Let's go, bud. It's only three more burpees. You can do this. You've got to finish if you think you're doing Spartan this fall. Those burpees aren't doing themselves. Down. Out. Pushup. In. Up! Get those pushups down low!"

Kelsey James channeled her inner boot camp instructor, her voice firm and commanding as she trained her client, Favian. As a master personal trainer and nutrition coach in Oakview, California, Kelsey took great pride in helping her clients achieve their desired results. This morning, however, Favian wasn't particularly amused by Kelsey's enthusiastic impersonation. With a determined frown etched on his face and sweat dripping from his brow he powered through the final burpees of his grueling workout. Out of breath, he sat on the bench next to Kelsey and reached for his water bottle. "You did a great job today, Favian. Way to push it."

"Thanks, Kels. I'm exhausted." Favian wiped his face with his towel and then proceeded to the locker room.

"Hey, Kelsey," Saffron, Fox's gym manager, said as she popped her head out the office door. "I have a new member who would like to do some sessions. I put her consultation on your calendar."

"Fabulous. Thanks, Saff."

Saffron, a beautiful Lebanese woman with long brown hair and the olive complexion that most women only dream of having, had worked at Fox Fitness since high school and ran and maintained the twenty-four-hour gym. When Kelsey joined Fox Fitness as a member eight years ago, they immediately hit it off, becoming best friends after a few years.

"You know your clients hate you," Justin, Kelsey's coworker and best guy friend, whispered into her ear as he walked by. Then he did his best Dr. Evil impersonation, "Wahahahaha!"

Justin Reed, a thirty-one-year-old transplant from Austin, Texas, fit right in at Fox. At six foot two inches tall and 187 pounds, Justin towered over Kelsey's five-foot-tall stature. When Justin moved to Oakview a little over a year and a half ago, he and Kelsey discovered they had the same taste in food and humor and quickly became friends. They made fun of each other and challenged one another, which kept the atmosphere in the gym alive. The members chimed in on their conversations, usually in the form of bantering across the gym floor. Their topics ranged from new fitness gear to food to the latest Netflix bingeworthy show.

Kelsey slugged Justin in the arm. "They love me once their six-pack shows up. I can't help it if I'm a bit pushy."

"A bit?" Justin said as he rolled his eyes and walked away.

Chapter 2

Sunday, September 11, 2022

Tina Scott wandered down the bustling aisles of the Oakview Farmers Market, her thoughts preoccupied with the surprising results of her DNA test. She moved past a stall displaying a rainbow of heirloom tomatoes, the earthy smell of the nearby flower stand mixing with the sweet scent of freshly baked pastries. The air was filled with the chatter of vendors and customers; the occasional laughter blended with the distant strumming of a street musician's guitar. Tina absentmindedly fingered a basket of ripe strawberries, her mind racing with questions. Could the test be wrong? How accurate were these things? Even with the vibrant surroundings, the whirlwind of thoughts swirled around in her mind.

Her phone rang. Her mom, Anna, was calling.

"Hi, Mama. What's up?" Tina said.

"Hi, sweetie. What are you doing right now?" Anna asked.

"I'm at the farmers' market getting some stuff to meal prep for this week. Kelsey said it would help me get even better results in the gym if I planned my meals ahead of time. She said to make sure I eat a lot of lean protein and veggies. I can deadlift 185 pounds now."

"That's my strong girl. Wow, you love training with her, don't you?"

"I do. Kelsey makes it fun. So, what's going on?"

"Well, I told you about that big work deal I just closed, right? I was thinking you and I could do a little celebration tonight. What do you think?"

"Sure! What did you have in mind?"

"Nothing big. Maybe we could cook a nice dinner together and watch a movie. I bought a bottle of the Taittinger champagne you like."

"That sounds great. Since I'm here at the market, I can pick something up."

"Wonderful! Okay, honey. I'll see you when you get home. I love you, Tina."

"Love you too, Mom."

As she made her way to the hummus booth, Tina looked up to see Kelsey and Justin standing in front of her.

"Hey, Tina! Are you getting some good stuff for meal prep like we talked about?" Kelsey said, picking over the tomatoes.

"Hi, Kelsey! Hi Justin! My mom just closed a big contract at work, so we will celebrate tonight by making something delicious. I was thinking of making a Mediterranean meal. I also picked up some zucchini and potatoes for meal prep." Tina eyed the freshly baked pita and hummus assortment on the table.

Tina's expression suddenly changed from happy and excited to a look of doom as she noticed her dad walking in her direction. *What is he doing here?*

Nick Scott came from behind Kelsey and walked toward Tina, his hair unkempt and his breathing elevated. He bumped into Kelsey's shoulder and then realized what he had done.

"Sorry, sorry," he said to Kelsey without looking directly at her.

"Tina, can we please just talk? Your mom hasn't been answering her phone. We need to sit down as a family to discuss this whole situation," Nick said.

"Dad! I told you. I don't want to talk about it. And maybe Mom doesn't want to either. Please just give us some room to breathe." Tina quickly gave the cashier money for her pita and hummus. Hoping her dad wouldn't follow her, she rushed toward the parking lot, her emotions rising.

"But I..." he continued and followed her.

Kelsey turned to Justin and said, "I can't believe that was Mr. Scott. I hardly recognized him. He looked out of sorts. I wonder why Tina didn't want to talk to him."

Justin shrugged and said, "Maybe he's having a bad day."

"Let's head in that direction to make sure Tina got to her car okay."

Kelsey and Justin arrived at the parking lot and saw Tina a few yards away talking to Mr. Scott. She shook her head as he spoke, her arms up in the air in protest.

"What do you think they're saying?" Justin asked quietly.

"I don't know. But it doesn't look good. Let's walk slowly to the truck so we can intervene if she needs us," Kelsey replied.

Mr. Scott reached to grab Tina's arm. Justin was about to run over and help when Tina pulled away from her dad and got into her car. Mr. Scott yelled something at Tina as she sped away in her little red Ford Focus. Getting into an oversized Ram truck, Mr. Scott drove off in the same direction as Tina, leaving a cloud of dust in his wake.

Chapter 3

Sunday, September 11, 2022

Anna Scott arranged a beautiful bouquet on the kitchen counter. Her new client, San Dimas Security, was pleased with the consulting services her company provided. A gift card for dinner at Luceti's Restaurant came with the bouquet. Maybe she'd ask Leo out to dinner. This year had been rough on him. COVID had done a number on his company. And Mae hadn't been happy about his reduction in income either. Then again, Mae was never happy with anything.

Tina entered the kitchen and set her bag of goodies on the counter. She looked at her mom and sighed.

"What's wrong, honey?" Anna said.

"It's Dad. He made a scene at the farmers' market in front of Kelsey. It was so embarrassing. Why does our family have so much drama?"

"I'm sorry, Tina. I'll talk with your father later, okay? It's my fault. I thought about not telling him but didn't think it was right. Everything will be okay, honey. I promise." Anna reached over to give Tina a big hug, and Tina inhaled the notes of her mom's familiar perfume, bergamot and hinoki.

Tina looked at her mom and smiled. She knew her mom would make everything better.

Chapter 4

Tuesday, September 13, 2022

Tik ... tik ... tik ...

The hands of the clock appeared to move in slow motion as Kelsey paced the gym floor. There was no sign of Tina. She routinely arrived at least five to ten minutes before her sessions to warm up. The unsettled feeling in Kelsey's stomach got tighter. She picked her phone up and tried Tina again.

Ring. Ring. Ring.

"Hi, you've reached Tina Scott. Leave a message!" *Beep!*

Tina had never missed a session in five years and always responded to Kelsey's texts. Always. When Kelsey spoke with Tina the night of the farmers' market, Tina had apologized for walking away so quickly and not saying goodbye. She said she would tell Kelsey all about the crazy family drama the next time she saw her. Then, Tina sent Kelsey a text asking if she could reschedule her Monday afternoon session to today.

At five foot three inches tall and 120 pounds, Tina was a little powerhouse. The Olympic barbell was her best friend, and she even named her favorite bar, Joe. Overheard in the gym one evening when the gym's macho man, Jimmy, was trying to hit on her: "No thanks, I have a date with Joe." Jimmy was *that* guy—all upper body with toothpick legs and no butt. All gyms probably have a Jimmy.

Over the years, Kelsey and Tina had grown closer. A few weeks ago, Saffron had one of her girls' nights and asked Kelsey to invite Tina. They, along with Charlie, another Fox trainer, had a blast. Saffron had made way too much food and by the end of the night, they were all giddy from sangria and tapas.

As Justin re-racked a pair of dumbbells, Kelsey walked up to him with worry written all over her face and sighed.

"Weren't you supposed to train Tina tonight?" he asked her.

"She didn't show. Justin, I'm worried about her."

Justin wrapped his arm around Kelsey's shoulders and said, "Aww, don't worry, Kelsey Sue. I'm sure she's fine. Maybe she just got her days mixed up."

Kelsey nodded. "I hope so." But deep down, she knew this was not the case.

Chapter 5

Tuesday night, September 13, 2022

"Chinese?" Kelsey asked.

Justin nodded as he grabbed the dog leash and clipped it to the collar of Kelsey's three-year-old basset hound, Finley. Kelsey took her phone and placed their usual order: one order of chicken gyoza, General Tsao's spicy chicken, crispy Hong Kong-style chow mein with extra bok choy and char-siu, and an order of mu shu pork. Then, she tried Tina again.

"Hi, you've reached ..." Kelsey hung up and texted Tina. *Please call or text me back. I need to know you're okay.*

"Brrr!" Justin and Finley returned less than five minutes later. "It's cold out there. Fin did his thing and headed straight back."

A few minutes later, the doorbell rang.

"That was fast!" Justin said, jumping up from the couch to open the door. Kelsey headed to the kitchen to grab plates and utensils.

"Kelsey! Kelsey, come here!" Justin yelled. "Quick!"

"What's going on?" Kelsey yelled back, wondering what the five-alarm fire could be.

Kelsey rushed in to see what Justin was clamoring about. As she reached the front door, her jaw dropped.

Chapter 6

Tina was standing on Kelsey's doorstep covered in blood. The front of her shirt, the bottom half of her jeans, and her hands looked like she had stepped out of a horror movie. Her chest heaved as she struggled to catch her breath. Her face was pale and her eyes wide, projecting a mix of fear and exhaustion. Each breath was a ragged gasp, her body trembling from the effort. Bending over, Tina wrapped her arms tightly around her torso as if trying to hold herself together.

"Justin, call an ambulance!" Kelsey barked as she pulled Tina inside.

"No, no, don't call. I'm okay. It's not mine," Tina managed to say in between breaths.

"I'm sorry, Kels. I didn't know where to go."

"It's okay. Start from the beginning. You're safe now. Where is the blood coming from? Here, sit down."

Kelsey directed Tina to the couch. "Tell me what happened."

Justin handed Tina a bottle of water and a towel. He then gave Kelsey a pair of kitchen gloves. She slipped them on. With permission, Kelsey carefully peeled Tina's flannel shirt off. The blood was mainly on the outside of Tina's clothes and Kelsey couldn't see any visible wounds.

"Hey there, slow down a little. Let's take more deep breaths." Kelsey crouched down and made eye contact with Tina. Immediately, Kelsey felt the pain in Tina's eyes. *What is she not telling us?* Kelsey guided Tina through the box breathing technique they used at the gym when Tina's heart rate got high after a heavy lift.

Tina looked up at Kelsey and said, "I need to go. I can't be here. I shouldn't have come here. I'm so sorry." She stood to leave.

"No, wait, stay here. Justin and I can help you," Kelsey said. "Whose blood is this, Tina?

Does it have something to do with what happened at the farmers' market? Are you in danger?"

"No. I mean, I don't know. I think my mom is dead," Tina said.

"What do you mean you think your mom is dead?" interjected Justin. "Where is she?"

"When I got home, she was on the entryway floor. Her eyes were closed, and there was a puddle of blood underneath her. I started shaking her gently and telling her to wake her up, but she didn't move. She wasn't breathing, and I couldn't find a pulse. I tried doing CPR and I kept leaning over her to see if I could hear her breathing. Then I thought I heard a noise in the house and I got spooked. I froze. I got so scared I ran. She's dead. I know she is. This blood. It's my mom's."

"We have to call nine-one-one," said Justin, "Kelsey, call your dad while I do that."

Kelsey dialed her dad's office line first, "You've reached the desk of Randy James, Oakview Chief of Police ..." She hung up and tried his cell phone. Randy picked up in two rings.

"Hey, Dad, my client Tina just found her mom dead at their house. Justin's on the phone with nine-one-one. She's here with me and Justin at my place right now."

"What? Kelsey, are you okay?" Randy exclaimed.

"Yes, Dad. I'm fine. Are you still at the station?"

"Not in Oakview. I'm in the city. I had a late meeting with the chief of San Francisco. We were just about to grab a drink. I'll head down to the crime scene right now. You stay where you are. Lock the doors and windows. I'll have dispatch catch me up on the situation on my drive home. Are you sure you're okay?"

"Dad, I'm fine. Tina's shaken up. Justin and I are going to stay here with her."

"Officers are on their way here and to Tina's house," Justin said, loud enough for Randy to hear.

"Okay, just stay put and do what the officers tell you. I'm on my way," Randy said.

"Hey, Kels. The nine-one-one dispatcher said someone already called it in before us." Justin said. "Tina, did you call them when you were trying to revive your mom? Did anyone see you run from your house?"

"No, I was too busy trying to give my mom CPR that I didn't call nine-one-one. Wow, I'm such an idiot," Tina said, slapping her forehead with her palm. "I don't remember seeing anyone outside when I left. I shut the front door and then sprinted straight here."

"Let's call your dad before the police get here," Kelsey said.

Tina nodded, her hand shaking as she dialed her dad's number.

"Hey, you've reached Nick Scott. You know the drill."

"Dad, it's me. Call me back. Mom's dead. Please call me back. I don't know what to do. Just call me, okay?" Tina's voice quivered as she left the message.

A sudden knock at the door jolted all three of them out of their seats. Justin walked over to answer it. The restaurant delivery driver handed him their order. In all the excitement, they had forgotten about their Chinese food.

Justin placed the bag of food on the table, then turned to Tina and said, "I have a question. If you shut the door behind you, how would someone know to call nine-one-one?"

Chapter 7

Tuesday, September 13, 2022

Murders didn't happen in Oakview every day. There were traffic stops, or drunk and disorderlies. There had also been domestic disputes. Oakview was a town of about twenty-six thousand people and was located a few cities south of San Francisco. With a smattering of mom-and-pop shops, Oakview had that small-town feel people loved.

Two Oakview police officers entered Kelsey's condo and introduced themselves as Officer Sanchez and Officer O'Donnell. After they asked Kelsey and Justin a few questions about the evening's events, the officers allowed them to sit with Tina during her interview.

Officer Sanchez: Okay, Ms. Scott, can you start from the beginning?

Tina: I came home at about 7:45, and the house was dark. Usually, my mom is home by then, so it was weird that the lights were all off.

Officer Sanchez: And for the record, your mom's name is?

Tina: Anna Scott.

Officer Sanchez: So, you came home. What did you do?

Tina: I put my key in the front door, but it was already unlocked. The little lamp in the front area that turns on automatically when it's dark wasn't on. As soon as I opened the door, I saw my mom lying there, the lamp broken on the floor next to her. I turned my phone flashlight on because it was so dark and closed the front door behind me. I thought maybe she fell and hit her head, but there was a lot of blood. The right side of her face looked like someone had bashed it in, and her neck was at a weird angle. I tried to wake her up and check for her pulse, but there wasn't one. I tried doing CPR compressions, but it didn't seem to do anything. I held her in my arms and started rocking back and forth crying. I kept checking to see if she was breathing, but there still wasn't anything. Then I thought I heard a shuffling sound. I got spooked, so I ran here. At first, I just ran and didn't know where to go. I felt like someone was watching me. I kept looking behind me. I could feel my body shivering and my teeth chattering. Then I remembered Kelsey lived close by.

Officer Sanchez: Is there anyone you can think of who would want to hurt your mom?

Tina: No. I can't think of anyone. My mom is a good person. She and my dad are divorced, but they get along fine now that they're not together. My mom is kind of an introvert. She doesn't have a lot of friends, but I don't think she has any enemies either.

Officer Sanchez: Was your mom acting strange or out of the ordinary the past few days?

Tina: No, not at all.

Officer Sanchez: Do you know where your dad is?

Tina: He's probably home at his apartment or something right now. He usually gets off work at six or seven. I tried calling him, but he didn't answer.

Officer Sanchez: We want to know more about the people who were close to your mom. The more we know, the more we can ask better questions to get to the bottom of this. Are there any friends or coworkers you can think of who would do something like this?

Tina: We have a big family. She's close to my aunts and uncles, but other than that, it was just me and her.

Officer Sanchez: We'll speak to all your family members individually. Maybe you can help us make a list of them. We'll start with your dad because he's part of your immediate family. We're not accusing him of anything. We just want to talk to him.

Tina (nodding): Okay, I can give you his phone number.

Officer Sanchez: Great. And don't worry. We'll be asking everyone we can think of who may be able to tell us more about your mom and the people she knew. We're going to find out who did this, Tina.

Tina (sniffling): Okay. Thank you.

Officer Sanchez: Thank you for answering our questions. We appreciate it. I think that's it for now, Tina. You've been very helpful.

Tina (sobbing quietly): Can I go see her?

Officer Sanchez: Officers are on the scene right now, so you can't go over there just yet. We'll keep in contact and let you know. [Turning to Kelsey] In the meantime, can she stay here?

We need to know she's in a safe spot. Here's my card, I'm Officer Sanchez. Detective Hart and I will be heading up this investigation. If you think of anything else, call me.

Kelsey: Of course. Yes, she can spend the night in my guest room.

[End of interview].

***

Justin gently took Kelsey aside to speak to her privately in the kitchen. Tina sat on the couch petting Finley with one hand, her head in her other hand.

"I'm going to Tina's house to see if I can find anything out," Justin quietly said.

"Good idea. I feel so bad she can't see her mom. Poor kid. I can't even imagine. I'll stay here with her and get her cleaned up," Kelsey said.

"Okay. I'll keep you posted."

***

Justin returned one hour later. He looked exhausted, and Kelsey pulled him over to the couch.

"What happened?" she asked.

"Is Tina sleeping?" Justin asked, looking around the condo.

"Yes, she's sleeping. She showered and I gave her some pajamas and a change of clothes for tomorrow. We did a shot of whiskey to calm our nerves. When I checked on her a few minutes ago, she was out like a light."

"This is so traumatic. I don't know what I would have done if I found my mom dead. There were three police cars, two fire trucks, an ambulance, and the coroner's van," Justin said.

"I wonder what happened. Did Anna fall and hit her head, or did someone attack her? Did she feel like she was in danger before this happened? Was it a random attack? Was anything stolen from the house? Does this have anything to do with the family stuff Tina has been dealing with?" Kelsey said.

Justin yawned and looked at his watch. "I don't know but I'm darn tired. It's midnight, Kels. I've got to get some shuteye. Do you want me to stay here and sleep on the couch or will y'all be okay?"

"We'll be fine. You should probably head home, Jus. Be careful out there, though. After what happened tonight, we should all be uber aware of our surroundings. Thanks for staying here with us and checking on the scene at Tina's house. I appreciate it, and I know Tina does too."

"Of course. I'm happy to help. I'll see you in the morning," Justin said as he stood up to leave.

As Kelsey locked the front door, she was glad she had Justin to help and felt secure because he lived only two blocks away. She thought *This doesn't seem like a burglary gone wrong or some accident. Which means there's a killer on the loose.*

Chapter 8

Tuesday, September 13, 2022

Chief Randy James: At approximately 7:45 p.m., upon arriving home to the house where she and her mother live, Tina Scott, daughter of Anna Scott, claims she found her mother unresponsive in the hallway of their home. She then started CPR compressions but could not get a pulse. Tina says she fled the scene after that because she was afraid for her own life and because she believed the killer might have still been in the home. At 7:50 p.m., we received a call from an anonymous person stating that Ms. Anna Scott was deceased in her home at 27 Watercrest Way. The anonymous caller hung up immediately after disclosing this information with no available callback number. We will conduct a formal investigation, which will include all family members, close friends, and acquaintances of the deceased. If you or anyone you know has information in conjunction with the death of Anna Scott, please call the Oakview Police Department Tipline at 800-345-9779. We will continue to update the public with any necessary information. Thank you.

Chapter 9

Wednesday, September 14, 2022

"Wake up!" Justin yelled across the gym. Kelsey's eyes were half shut and she was dragging.

"How are you so chipper this morning?" Kelsey said as she came over and lay down on a gym mat, arms and legs outstretched. "I'm going to take a nap right here. Go get me a blanket."

Justin held up his massive thermos of coffee. "Wanna cup o' joe? I made some extra strong java this morning to wake us up. It might help. I've had four cups already, and I'm awake!"

"You're so wired, Justin. Four cups? I've had two cups already, and now I'm just tired and jittery. And I need to go pee every five minutes. I don't think more coffee is the answer."

The front door of the gym buzzed to allow a gym member access. Kelsey and Justin turned to see who had entered.

"Hey, guys," Tina said softly and Kelsey sat up on her mat.

"Hey, Tina," Justin said, "How are you feeling?"

Kelsey got up and gave Tina a big hug. "What are you doing here? You should be resting."

"I lay in bed for a while this morning. I'm still in shock and there's a knot at the pit of my stomach. I wish I could have done something to save my mom. Also, I still can't get ahold of my dad. His assistant said he didn't come into the office today and he's not answering his cell. I came here because I didn't want to be alone. Is it okay if I hang out on the elliptical and listen to music? I'm so anxious right now."

"Of course. You're always welcome here," Kelsey said. "Do you think your dad went on a business trip and forgot to tell you?"

"I don't know, but he usually has his cell phone on him. Thank you for helping me last night, you guys. I don't know what I would have done without you."

"Of course. We're both here for you. Any word from the police?" Kelsey said.

"They called me this morning and said they would keep me posted. They said I could go home and get some of my things but that I should think about staying with a relative or friend for the time being."

"You can stay with me for as long as you'd like. We can go together and pick up your things later," Kelsey said.

"Thank you so much, Kelsey," Tina said as she stepped onto the elliptical.

The gym door opened, letting in a small rush of air, and Favian walked in.

"Hey, Kelsey, you'll be proud of me. I did well with my food this weekend, and I didn't drink any beer. It helped that I was at my parents' house helping my dad with projects. We rebuilt the deck, and my dad noticed that my physique looked a lot different. Plus, I'm stronger and have more energy."

"Hey, Favian," Kelsey said, with a small smile, "That's great."

"Are you okay?" Favian asked, quickly noticing Kelsey's somber mood.

Kelsey looked at him and took a deep breath. "Yeah, sorry, something happened last night, so I was up late. Sorry if I seem distracted today. Thanks for asking." Although last night's events still had Kelsey rattled, she knew it was time to get refocused and get to work. Her clients needed her.

"Uh oh. I hope everything will be okay. Let me know if there's anything I can do to help."

"Thanks, Favian. I appreciate it. Ready to workout?"

"Sure, I wanted to show you something. My buddy showed me this exercise on social media. Could we try it? I'd like to know if I'm doing it right. I don't remember what it's called but I have saved it in my Instagram," Favian said.

"Great. Pull up the video so I can see it."

Favian showed his phone to Kelsey. "Nice, the anti-gravity press. This is a great exercise. It's much harder than it looks."

"My buddy said he tried it, and he could hardly do it. But also, he doesn't have a trainer. At least not one as awesome as you. You're the best trainer I've ever had, Kels."

The corners of Kelsey's mouth lifted as she laughed and rolled her eyes at Favian. "Very funny. I'm the only trainer you've ever had. We're still doing burpees today."

Favian laughed, "I knew I could make you smile! You had me worried for a minute there, Kels. The last time I saw you with such a serious look on your face was the time you gave up caffeine for three days."

They both chuckled at the memory but stopped as they heard a commotion coming from the front of the gym.

"What are you doing here?" Tina yelled. The members and staff turned to look as a man quickly snatched Tina off the elliptical and ran outside.

"C'mon, Tina, I wouldn't have to do this if you just cooperated. Stop it," the man said in a low voice.

Wearing a blue and white Adidas tracksuit and white sneakers, the man was tall and had curly, dark brown hair with a large mole on his left temple. He was also wearing a COVID face mask. Tina was kicking but her screams were muffled by the man's hand.

Justin ran after them, but a black SUV had been ready and waiting outside with the door open. The man shoved Tina into the backseat, jumped in behind her, and closed the door as the SUV drove off. The driver was wearing sunglasses and a black baseball cap. Kelsey quickly took her phone out to take a picture of the license plate, but the SUV had driven off so fast, the picture turned out blurry.

Justin jumped in his truck and sped off. As Kelsey ran back into the gym, she passed the elliptical Tina had been on and noticed Tina's phone on the holder. The screen showed Tina's AirPods were still connected to the phone.

"Saff!! Saff!!" Kelsey yelled, holding up Tina's phone.

Saffron looked at Kelsey who was running frantically toward her and pointed to the phone in her hand as she spoke to the emergency dispatcher. "Yes, he grabbed her and ran outside. He put her in a black SUV. Her name is Tina Scott. Okay, let me get you that from our gym database. Hold on one second."

As Saffron gave the police Tina's information, Kelsey tried to guess the passcode to the phone. She knew if she could unlock it, she could use the friend finder app to see where Tina's AirPods pinged.

"They'll be here within the hour. I gave them Tina's name, address, phone number, and her dad's number. He's listed as her emergency contact," Saffron told Kelsey as she hung up with the operator. "Is that her phone?"

"Seriously? Someone just got kidnapped and it's going to take an hour? I'm trying to get into her phone to see if the app will find her location from her AirPods. I've tried her birthday, birth year, and the obvious one, two, three, four, but none of those worked. I'm calling my dad."

Randy's office and cell numbers both went straight to voice mail, so Kelsey texted him, *Tina kidnapped. Call ASAP.*

***

Forty minutes later, Justin returned to the gym, a trickle of sweat running down his brow as he asked Kelsey if there had been any news. Unfortunately, even with the Bay Area commute traffic, the kidnappers had gotten too much of a head start on him.

Fifteen minutes later, the police arrived. Saffron gave them a copy of the camera footage from the gym. Kelsey handed over Tina's phone and told the officers that if they could get into it, they could ping her Air Pods to see where she was. The officers looked at her as if she were speaking in tongues. Kelsey tried to call her dad again, and again, it went to voicemail.

Chapter 10

Wednesday, September 14, 2022

C hief Randy James: Tina Scott, daughter of Anna Scott, the woman who was found deceased last night, has been abducted. Here is the footage we've recovered from Fox Fitness twenty-four-hour gym in Oakview.

[Video plays]

If anyone has any information regarding the whereabouts of Tina Scott or her assailant, please call the Oakview Police Department at 800-345-9779.

Chapter 11

Wednesday, September 14, 2022

As Kelsey and Justin moved along the cobblestone path behind Tina's house, the trees swayed gently in the moonlight. The air was chilly and Kelsey shivered as they approached. Tina's two-story house backed up to a large grassy area. This area of Oakview was full of lush, tree-lined streets and beautifully manicured lawns. The front yards were decorated with gnomes, ponds, and colorful flowers which gave the neighborhood a unique charm.

As they snuck around the front of Tina's house, Justin and Kelsey tried to avoid setting off the security light sensors by staying low to the ground. The ends of the yellow police caution tape flapped in the breeze on the front porch. They decided to enter through the back of the house. Justin handed Kelsey a pair of rubber gloves, and she used an old Visa gift card to open the back door lock. Kelsey, having grown up with a police officer for a dad, had learned many useful skills from her father. As a teen, she had inadvertently helped him to solve a case he was working on when he was a detective. As she struggled with the lock, she accidentally knocked something down, and Justin picked it up. It was a phone with a black Labrador Retriever on the lock screen.

"We're not even in yet, and we've found a clue," Kelsey said. "That's a good sign." As the door creaked open, Kelsey whispered loudly, "Got it!"

Using Kelsey's phone flashlight, they scanned the room. The kitchen was a large, open concept with a textured stone floor and dark wood cabinets.

"This fridge is a Sub-Zero. Expensive," Justin remarked as he opened the refrigerator door. "I worked for a contractor in Austin. These things start at eleven thousand dollars. What did Tina's mom do for a living?"

"Finance, maybe? I remember Tina saying she closed a big deal recently."

As they made their way into the front hallway and living room, Kelsey noticed the little lamp Tina mentioned during her police interview. Police number markers were scattered around the area, each marking something significant to the crime scene.

Justin ascended the carpeted staircase with Kelsey close behind. The tan carpet was worn in the middle of each step, and a few of the steps creaked under their weight. As Kelsey stepped onto the landing, a long squeak and a shuffle echoed through the hall. They stopped dead in their tracks as a door clicked shut and a lock turned. Kelsey turned off her flashlight. They would have to rely on the moonlight streaming through the windows to guide them to the first bedroom. The door was slightly ajar. Kelsey and Justin slipped through, careful not to make any noise, and stood frozen, listening for sounds from downstairs.

Two minutes felt like an eternity, yet there didn't seem to be any more movement from downstairs. As Justin stood guard at the bedroom door, Kelsey quietly looked through the room. The patchwork quilt on the bed was undisturbed. There was an empty water glass on the bedside table, along with a small stack of romance paperback novels. Kelsey carefully flipped through each book in case there was a hidden note or receipt in one of them but came up empty. The clothes were organized by color in the walk-in closet; the shoes in neat rows on the top shelf. A white shoebox sat on the floor of the closet. Kelsey opened it and peered inside. A collection of photos and cards filled the box. Kelsey tucked it under her arm. After one final look around the room, Kelsey crouched down to look under the bed but found only a few dust bunnies.

As Kelsey stood up, Justin whispered to her, "Stay here," as he peeked out the door to make sure the coast was clear and then walked out of the room. He waved her over and, keeping their backs flush with the wall, they slithered down the hallway until they reached the next bedroom door.

Kelsey took a quick peek over the banister and grabbed Justin's hand to pull him into the bedroom.

Spotting a large closet with louvered doors, she rushed over to it and pulled Justin in.

"There's a woman downstairs," Kelsey whispered. "What should we do?"

Justin shrugged and pulled her close, whispering, "Who do you think it could be? It wasn't a police officer, was it?"

Kelsey rolled her eyes at him. "I think I know what a police officer looks like. No, it was a woman with dark hair. I couldn't see what she was wearing. I could only see the top of her head."

The pair listened carefully. From the sound of it, there was a lot of opening and closing of drawers and cabinets. Silverware rattled and the refrigerator opened and closed. Kelsey and Justin sat like statues, wondering when the lady would leave. Suddenly, there was a loud vibrating sound. Kelsey and Justin jumped. The phone they found outside was buzzing in Justin's bag. Justin hurried to silence the call, shielding the light so he and Kelsey could check the caller ID. The screen said, "Aunt Mae." Suddenly, they could hear footsteps coming closer. Justin put the phone on silent and shoved it back in his bag.

"She's on the stairs," Kelsey whispered, huddling closer to Justin.

Justin grabbed Kelsey's hand and pulled her out of the closet and into the adjoining bathroom, where they carefully climbed into the tub behind the shower curtain. They could hear the woman enter the bedroom. The woman banged the closet door open and after shuffling around in it, moved hastily around the room, opening drawers. Kelsey and Justin held their breath and prayed she didn't enter the bathroom.

The woman exited the room, her footsteps getting quieter. Kelsey and Justin listened carefully and after a few seconds, heard a quick stomp, a grunt, and a clatter echo through the house. It sounded like it came from the bedroom next door.

"Thank God," the woman announced to no one in particular. She was clearly annoyed by something. The sound of her footsteps trailed down the stairs and out the front door.

Kelsey and Justin both sighed in relief as they climbed out of the tub.

"Wait, let's wait a few seconds to make sure she's not coming back," Justin said. Kelsey could see him counting down from ten to one silently. When he reached the end of the countdown, he whispered, "Okay, stay here. I'll go look."

Before Kelsey could stop him, he slid out the bedroom door.

Justin reappeared as quickly as he left.

"Coast is clear. There's no car outside."

Kelsey nodded and grabbed the box of photos. Then they scurried out the way they came.

Arriving back at Kelsey's condo, they found Finley fast asleep on the couch. Justin yawned and said, "Hey, what do you say we start working on this stuff tomorrow? I'm beat." He handed Kelsey the phone to put with the shoebox and she set it on the kitchen table.

"I'll charge the phone and start looking through the box. I'll write everything down in my notebook and we can go over it tomorrow. Go home and get some rest," she told him.

"You and your notebooks, Kelsey Sue," Justin said, shaking his head at her.

"You know I love my notebooks. And you'll see. It's going to help us find Tina. Now get outta here." Kelsey said, pushing Justin out the front door.

Closing the door behind her, Kelsey's thoughts turned dark again. She knew Anna's killer might also be Tina's kidnapper. She had to act fast to save her friend. Grabbing her notebook and pen, Kelsey opened the box and went to work.

Chapter 12

Thursday, September 15, 2022

The leaves of the oak trees swirled in shades of yellow, red, and orange as they drifted gently to the ground. Kelsey pulled up to the gym in her truck which she had named Chuckie, a lifted black Ford Raptor that now roared to a stop. She spotted her client, Sam, warming up on the treadmill through the large glass window. As she entered the cool, air-conditioned gym, the hum of equipment and the rhythmic thud of feet on treadmills greeted her.

"Hey, Sam," Kelsey said as she walked past him to the front desk. "Ready for your deadlift PR?"

"I sure am!" he said.

The look in Kelsey's eyes was intense as she focused on Sam's form. Sam killed his deadlift PR, lifting more than he ever had at 255 pounds.

"That felt amazing, Kelsey!" Sam said.

As they finished the rest of his training session, Kelsey and Sam spoke about his future goals as a video game developer and programmer.

"So, Kelsey, my company is developing this awesome new military game similar to Call of Duty. Your brother might like it. We'll have a beta test early next year, so maybe he'd like to come down to the office and give it a go," Sam told her.

"He would love that. I'm seeing him this weekend. I'll tell him about it." Brian, Kelsey's thirteen-year-old little brother, loved video games and sometimes played them online with Justin.

"Hey, so Sam, I have a small favor to ask you. You can say no if you don't feel comfortable doing it," Kelsey said.

"Sure, ask away. If it's a tech thing, I'm sure I can help you. Or refer you to someone who can."

"I have a phone I need to unlock. I need to find its owner. Could you look at it for me?"

"A phone? No problem. I'm working from home today. Do you want to meet at Café Blanco at around one?" Sam said.

"That's perfect. Thank you so much."

"Great. I'll see you then."

After her session with Sam, Kelsey hustled across the gym floor to Justin to give him the update.

"I get off at one. Can I meet you guys there?"

"Of course. I hope unlocking the phone will give us a clue as to who kidnapped Tina."

"Or who killed Anna."

Chapter 13

Thursday, September 15, 2022

K elsey squinted as her eyes adjusted to the bright sun. As she stepped out of Chuckie and into the parking lot of the quaint, family-owned café, she spotted Sam seated at a charming outdoor bistro table. As she approached, she took a deep breath, savoring the fresh air mixed with the aroma of brewing coffee.

Kelsey sat down across from Sam and handed him the phone. Sam immediately began to examine it, his fingers deftly poking, prodding, and swiping across the screen. After a few moments, he set the phone back down on the table.

"I've removed the password and facial recognition requirements," he explained. "You can open it anytime now."

Kelsey nodded in appreciation. "Thanks, Sam. Can you help me figure out who this phone belongs to? Justin and I found it outside Tina's house the other night."

"Is Tina your client who was kidnapped from the gym?" Sam asked and Kelsey nodded. "I heard about that. Pretty scary."

"It is. Justin and I went to her house late last night to look for clues. We found the phone on the back step."

"Playing detective, are we?" Sam said jokingly.

"Hey, guys!" Sam and Kelsey turned to see Justin walking over with a big smile.

"My man!" Sam got up to shake Justin's hand.

"What's up, Sam? Good to see you. Did Kelsey tell you how we broke into Tina's house to look for clues?"

"Wait, you *broke* in?" Sam said with a surprised look on his face.

"I had to go with her because I didn't want her to get in trouble. You know how she can get carried away with things," Justin said, and Kelsey threw a right hook to his shoulder. "Woman! It was shoulder day yesterday. That hurt!"

"Carried away with things? Kelsey James? No!" Sam said with a huge grin.

"Hey! I'm sitting right here," Kelsey said to the guys who cracked up again.

A server approached their table, a warm smile on her face and a notepad and pen in hand, ready to take their orders. Justin ordered a ham and cheese-stuffed crepe, his mouth watering at the thought of the savory filling. He added a cold brew coffee to his order. Kelsey scanned the menu one last time before she decided on the country potatoes and poached eggs.

"I've never seen someone who likes potatoes as much as Kelsey," Justin said.

"It's my favorite food! I've never met a potato I haven't liked," she replied.

Sam got to work, his expert fingers moving over the phone's screen. He began by showing Kelsey how to retrieve deleted texts and emails that could provide crucial clues about the phone's owner and their connection to Tina.

As Sam dove deeper, he showed Kelsey how to access the phone's location history. He highlighted the past locations the phone had visited, each dot on the map potentially holding a piece of the puzzle. Kelsey watched intently, absorbing the information. In the process, they discovered the phone was named "Jason's iPhone," a detail Kelsey made a note of, feeling a small glimmer of progress in their investigation.

Kelsey wrote Sam's instructions down step by step. Skimming the emails, they found out Jason's full name. Jason Crenshaw. With over 5,500 emails in his inbox, it would take a while to go through them. Kelsey noticed Jason's email mainly consisted of store advertisements and Alumni News from UCSF. Searching LinkedIn, Kelsey found a Jason Crenshaw who had UCSF listed as his college. Jason Crenshaw. Oakview, California. Current employer: Stanford University-Clinical Research Assistant. She moved on to his photo app. Jason's photo roll was less than impressive. There were only twenty-six pictures in total, but Kelsey now had an idea of what Jason looked like.

"Take pictures of the important information you find on the phone. If Jason gets a new phone, which I'm sure he will, this one will be wiped clean and the information will get ported over to his new phone. Better do that now," Sam advised.

Kelsey and Justin worked for the next two hours, siphoning through the information on the phone. They found out:

1. The phone's owner was Jason Crenshaw.

2. The "Mom" and "Dad" contacts didn't have names but did have phone numbers and the same address listed for both. The phone numbers both belonged to David Crenshaw.

3. A search for "David Crenshaw Oakview California" brought up several listings. One of which was a dentist in the area.

4. The "Aunt Mae" contact in his address book only had a phone number. After a quick reverse phone number lookup, Kelsey found out her last name was Eriksen. There was also a contact named "Uncle Leo" and his last name was also Eriksen.

5. The last visited locations on the iPhone were David Crenshaw's house, Tina's house, and Fox Fitness.

6. There were two texts back and forth between Jason and Tina on the night Anna was killed. The first was one from Jason to Tina and said, *5:00?* Tina had responded, *Sounds good. I've got to clear my head a bit.*

Chapter 14

Thursday, September 15, 2022

"Hey, Josh, I'm glad I ran into you. How are the shifts working out so far?" Randy said as he and Officer Josh DeLuca exited the police station. They stopped to chat next to one of the police cruisers.

"Everything is great, Chief. Thank you again for the opportunity to work for Oakview PD. This is a great town with a great police force. I'm happy to be a part of it. Back in Seattle, we didn't do as many community events as you do here. It's refreshing to meet the people of Oakview without them feeling like they're getting into trouble with a cop," Josh said.

"I know what you mean. And that's exactly why we do those events. We want people to feel comfortable around community service officers. We're here to keep the town and its people safe. Say, Josh, since you're new in town, I'd like to invite you over to my house this Sunday for brunch with my family. Say ten o'clock? My Joanna makes a mean French toast." Randy chuckled. "What do you say?"

"That sounds great, Chief. I would love to meet your family. What can I bring?"

"Just bring yourself. Joanna always makes plenty of food. Here, let me write down my address for you." Randy pulled his notebook and pen out of his breast pocket.

"Great. Thank you, sir. I'll see you then," Josh said as he took the slip of paper.

Randy looked up to see Kelsey and Justin walking in their direction.

"Hi, Dad!" Kelsey said. When she was little, Kelsey spent hours helping Randy with tasks such as fixing the car or gardening. She was underfoot all the time as his little helper, and he had taught her all sorts of cool tricks, like how to make a fire using sticks and a knife and how to get out of a hold if someone grabbed you from behind. As far as Randy was concerned, their father-daughter bond was solidified the first time he held her at the hospital.

"Hey, sweetie! I'd like you to meet our newest officer, Josh DeLuca. He was transferred here from Seattle about a month ago. Josh, this is my daughter Kelsey, and her friend Justin."

Strikingly handsome with dark brown hair and blue eyes, Kelsey noticed Josh's good looks and immediately blushed. *This guy looks like he works out. With the last name DeLuca, he's probably Italian.*

"Hi, Josh. Nice to meet you," Kelsey said, shaking his hand.

"How is the Bay Area compared to Seattle?" asked Justin.

"Honestly, the people here are a lot ruder than in Seattle, but the streets are much cleaner, so it seems to be balancing out." Josh chuckled. "I've only been here for a month so I really shouldn't judge yet. But so far so good. I like working for this department. Your dad's a great chief, Kelsey."

"You should hang out at the gym with us sometime. You look like you're a guy who works out. Fox is twenty-four hours," Justin said.

"I'll have to take you up on that offer. I've been meaning to find a gym that fits my schedule. A twenty-four-hour one would be perfect," Josh replied.

There was an uncomfortable silence before Kelsey finally said, "Well, it was nice to meet you. We're headed to the store to grab food for dinner. Justin's making his loaded burgers."

Randy leaned over and kissed Kelsey on the top of her head just like when she was little. "See you Sunday, kiddo. Love you."

She whispered to him, "Did you get the phone?" "Talk later, okay?" he whispered back.

***

"All right, all right. Who's ready for some loaded burgers?" Justin asked as they entered the store.

"This girl!" Kelsey said as she pointed her thumbs at herself. "Can you make Tzatziki to go with it?"

"I sure can, Kelsey Sue! How about you get the tater tots and meat? A pound of ground lamb and a pound of grass-fed ground beef. I'll meet you in produce."

***

The two arrived at Kelsey's condo twenty minutes later, and while Justin cooked, Kelsey continued to review the information on Jason's phone. Justin hummed while cooking, then plated the food. Of course, he made sure to give Kelsey extra tots. Finley even got his own mini loaded burger with meat and tots only. Setting the food down on the coffee table, he grabbed a bottle of Syrah from Kelsey's wine rack, noting it would go well with the spices in the burgers. As they dug into their meal, Kelsey said, "This burger is so good, Justin. I hadn't realized I was this hungry."

"I'm glad you like it. It's a Justin Reed specialty, and you are one of the only people who has ever had the pleasure of eating one," Justin said, grinning at the look on Kelsey's face.

"Okay, so we need to find out who this Jason guy is. Maybe he knows where Tina is. Or maybe he's trying to find out where she is, just like us. His phone couldn't have been sitting under the back stoop for long. He must have dropped it there after the murder. Otherwise, the police would have found it," Justin said, thinking out loud.

Kelsey picked the phone back up only to realize it had been wiped clean. Jason must have ported his number over to a new phone. She would have to make do with the information she took from it. Pivoting, she moved onto the shoebox. Although she had gone through a few of the items the night before, she had been tired and probably wasn't as thorough as she should have been.

Starting at the top of the pile, Kelsey and Justin looked at each photo meticulously, several of which had dates on them. Most of the photos were of Tina from infanthood to present day. Halfway down the box was a worn photograph with "2002 Jason and Tina" written on the back. Tina was three years old. Jason looked six or seven. Below that, were more photos of Anna with different people. One photo was of Anna at a party with multicolored balloons; she held a very little Tina in her arms. As she meticulously looked through the photos, Kelsey felt her eyes start to glaze over. She looked at the time. Nine-thirty. They had been going through the box for almost three hours. The next photo she picked up was of Tina's dad, Nick, and three other people. The back of the photo said "1995, Abby, Mae, Nick, and Franklin." Mae? As in, Aunt Mae?

"Hey," Justin said, and Kelsey jumped. Justin laughed, "You must be finding some good clues in that box. I was calling you from the kitchen to see if you wanted to open another bottle."

"There are so many random photos. I don't want to miss anything. Another bottle would be great. I think I'm starting to get somewhere with these. Look, here's Tina with Jason. I just wish I could figure out his part in all of this. Do you want to open the bottle of Coppola Claret that Sylvia got me for Christmas?"

"Sure. Hey, do you think I could spend the night in your guest room tonight since we've been drinking?"

"Of course. You're always welcome to crash here. Linens are clean in the guest room."

Kelsey stumbled upon a baseball card with the name "Leo Eriksen" emblazoned on the front. It resembled a vintage Topps baseball card, complete with player stats. Leo Eriksen. Pitcher. *This is Uncle Leo*, Kelsey realized and she took a minute to examine the man's rugged features. He was a large guy with a square jawline, dark brown hair, and piercing blue eyes. Something about him seemed familiar to Kelsey but she couldn't pinpoint what. Despite sharing the same last name, Mae and Leo looked nothing alike. Mae had long, black hair and dark eyes. Could they be married?

Digging deeper, Kelsey found a photo of a sweet newborn baby. *This must be Tina*, she thought. She noticed the photo didn't resemble the typical hospital newborn photos like the ones her parents had of her and Brian. Instead, it was a Polaroid of the baby swaddled in a gray blanket, lying on a brown shag carpet. The picture was slightly faded, with "9/90" faintly penciled on the back.

As she pondered these discoveries, Justin poured her another glass of wine. The rich, crimson liquid swirled in the glass and added a touch of warmth and comfort to the moment.

"Hey, Justin. Look at this," she said, holding up the photo. "This can't be Tina. It says 9/90 on the back. As in September 1990."

Justin and Kelsey looked at each other wide-eyed. Did Anna have a child other than Tina?

Chapter 15

Friday, September 16, 2022

"Oh, my buddy!" Saffron cooed. Anytime Kelsey brought Finley into the gym, Saffron doted over him. She set out his water bowl and toys. He even had a bed Saffron bought him last Christmas. Finley pounced, putting his little paws on her leg. She bent down and gave him a big hug. He returned the love with a big lick on her chin. Saffron giggled and took his leash, leading him to the front desk area. "Okay, Fin, what are we going to do today?" Saffron said as they walked away, his tail wagging a mile a minute.

"Well, I guess I don't have to worry about him for the day," Kelsey laughed.

A few minutes later, Kelsey's first client of the day, Caroline, walked in. Caroline was in her late seventies and was as fit as a fiddle. She trained three days a week and went to barre classes with her friends twice a week.

"Kelsey, honey, I wanted to give you this," Caroline said as she pulled out a little white jar from her purse. "It's that collagen cream I told you about the other day. Look at how smooth it's made my neckline. You can never start too early with good skincare!" She lifted her chin and pointed to her neck.

"Wow, thanks, Caro. I'm excited to try it. Right now, I just use a cleanser, toner, and light moisturizer. Sometimes I'll splurge on a Vitamin C serum, too," Kelsey said.

"Well, this cream is like a miracle worker. You can use it in the morning and before bedtime. Make sure you put some on your neck and décolleté, too. The wrinkles will start to creep into those spots before you know it. Trust me. I'm an old woman with a lot of old friends, so I know."

"What are you talking about, Caro? You're not old! You've got more energy than a thirty-year-old!"

"Oh, Kelsey that's why I love you so much. You make me feel young again! Speaking of young, has my daughter Audrey contacted you about training yet? I told her you're very busy, so she needs to contact you ASAP to claim a spot. I gave her your card. She's very thin and she doesn't have much muscle so you'll have to start easy on her."

"Of course. We'll figure out her goals and fitness level first. I haven't heard from her yet, but I'm sure she'll contact me soon. Thanks for the referral."

Two hours later, Saffron and Finley walked over to where Kelsey was standing, scrolling on her phone.

"Hey, guys," Kelsey said, looking up at Saffron and then bending over to give her pup a pat on the head. "I was just about to come up to the front to say hi. I was going over some of the notes I had written to myself about Tina's kidnapping.

"Any new findings on where she could be?" Saffron asked Kelsey.

"Well, I'm annoyed I haven't heard back from my dad about Tina's phone. They could have found her by now if they pinged her Air Pods the day she was kidnapped," Kelsey said and then caught Saffron up on what she and Justin found the night before.

"Did you say Jason and Tina know each other? And that his aunt's name is Mae Eriksen? Mae does a lot of work with the Rotary Club. I only know because my mom does Rotary, too. They organize different things like food drives and some community 5Ks. Remember when I ran that 5K last summer through the park?"

"I do." Kelsey scribbled the information down in her notebook. "So, you know Mae Eriksen? Do you know Jason Crenshaw? Or David Crenshaw?"

"I know Mae is married to a guy named Leo. I don't know any Crenshaws, though."

"Okay, that makes sense. I found this old baseball card in Anna's stuff with the name Leo Eriksen on it. He must have played for either a college team or the minor leagues back in the day. The card looked pretty old."

"I've never met Leo. And I've only seen Mae a couple of times at different functions." Saffron added.

"Mae and Leo Eriksen are Jason's aunt and uncle. We need to figure out how this is all connected to Tina," Kelsey said, thinking out loud. "We should draw a family tree to get a visual of who all the family members are. There was a picture of Abby, Mae, Nick, and Franklin. If I were to guess, maybe they're siblings? I don't know. We'll start with family and then close friends. For as long as I've known Tina, she's never had too many friends. And she doesn't talk about her family much except for her mom and dad."

"That's a good idea. I'll start drawing the family tree, and we can start filling in the blanks. I'll also see if I can find some pictures of her family members online," Saffron said.

With almost half an hour until her next client, Kelsey took Fin outside for a quick bathroom break. Returning to the gym, she saw Justin training his client, Kelly, a 250-pound body-builder who would scare anyone in a dark alley. Kelsey walked over as Kelly racked the barbell. He held up a hand to give her a high-five. "Hey! How's my little Irish sister doing?"

Kelsey smiled. "Doing good, Kelly. How's life?"

"I can't complain. This guy's got me lifting the heaviest I've ever done without the drugs. I feel great! Plus, did I tell you I'm getting married?"

"Congratulations! I'm so happy for you. Bring your fiancée in so we can all meet her."

"For sure. We're planning the wedding for next June. You and Justin are both invited. I wouldn't even be able to see my wedding day if it wasn't for this guy," Kelly said, tapping Justin on the shoulder.

Kelly was one of Justin's first clients at Fox. Kelly weighed around 350 pounds and had dangerously high blood pressure due to his use of anabolic steroids. His heart was so severely damaged that he ended up in the ICU after a massive heart attack, and the doctors didn't think he would survive. Miraculously, he pulled through.

The doctor advised Kelly to quit the steroids, adopt a healthy nutrition plan, and get a trainer to adjust his gym workouts.

Almost a year later, with Justin's guidance and support, Kelly had lost nearly 100 pounds. He could now lift heavy weights again, demonstrating remarkable progress and resilience.

After giving Justin a synopsis of her conversation with Saffron, Justin said, "Well, aren't you just a regular Nancy Drew? I can see it on your office door in bright lights, 'Kelsey Sue, Sleuth Detective'."

Kelsey was about to roll her eyes and make a smart-aleck remark when her phone rang.

Chapter 16

Friday, September 16, 2022

An hour later, Chuckie rumbled up Ralston Avenue and pulled into the Baymont Shopping Center. The parking lot was full even though it was midday on a Friday. People were most likely gearing up for the weekend. The grocery store in the shopping center had a wonderful selection of gourmet meats, cheeses, and wines. Kelsey and Finley arrived at Riverdog Restaurant, where Randy was already seated.

"Hi, sweetheart! How's my girl? Thanks for meeting me on such short notice," Randy said, as he reached down to pet Finley, "Hey boy, how ya doing?"

"No problem. I was talking to Justin when you called. Any news on Tina's mom's case or Tina's kidnapping? Were you able to ping her AirPods?"

"That's one of the reasons I wanted to chat with you. Tina's phone pinged her Air Pods to a location bubble in the Aragon district in San Mateo. She could be anywhere in the bubble. That's the good news. We think we know where she is. The bad news is that we lost transmission yesterday evening. There hasn't been a murder in Oakview for a long time. Or a kid-napping, for that matter. We've got our hands full with this one. Right now, we're trying to get ahold of a kid named Jason Crenshaw. He's about your age, maybe a little younger. Do you know him?"

Kelsey gasped, choking on her water. Just then, the server came over, and she could hardly focus on what he said. *Why does my dad need to know if I know Jason?*

"I'll have the BLT with fries," Randy said as Kelsey gave him a side-eye. He shouldn't be eating fried or high-sodium foods because of his high blood pressure. "I know, I know. Not the healthiest. I need to take a page out of your book and improve my nutrition."

"And exercise," she added.

"And exercise," he repeated.

"I'll have the wild-caught salmon with lemon and capers, and a side of mashed potatoes, please," Kelsey said to their server and then turned back to Randy. "So, who is Jason Crenshaw?"

"I was hoping you know him. He's Tina's cousin."

Kelsey nodded. This all made sense now. She reached for her notebook and pen from her bag. "What?" she said.

"You and your notebooks. You're like a regular Nancy Drew," Randy laughed, his small beer belly bouncing up and down.

Kelsey rolled her eyes. "So, Jason is Tina's cousin? On which side? His last name isn't Scott. Is his mom related to her dad? Or is her mom related to Jason's dad?"

"Whoa, whoa, slow down there. Jason's parents are Abby Scott Crenshaw and David Crenshaw. David is a dentist here in Oakview. Several of our officers go to him for dental work."

"Abby Scott? Jason's mom is Tina's dad's sister?"

"Yes," he said. "We pulled up Tina's cell phone records, and she was in contact with Jason the week before her mom was killed and the day of. Detective Hart has been trying to track the guy down but according to his employer, he's been out of town for the past few days."

As Kelsey contemplated whether to tell Randy about Jason's phone, he said, "Kelsey? What are you not telling me?"

"Fine. I have Jason's phone. But it's been shut down. I don't know him, but Justin and I snuck into Tina's house and found his phone outside on the back stoop. Then we hid in a closet because a woman came in. She seemed like she was looking for something, but we didn't know what. I took the phone, and a friend unlocked it and found out it was Jason's. Do you think Jason knows where she's at?"

"Kelsey Sue James! You did what? You broke into the house? You know that's against the law. You could have gotten yourself in some serious trouble. Now, tell me again what you know. Let me be the one to take notes this time." Randy took his police notebook out.

"Abby and David are Tina's uncle and aunt? On the phone, there was also an Aunt Mae and Uncle Leo. So, are they Tina's uncle and aunt, too?" Kelsey asked.

"Yes. Mae, Abby, and Nick are all siblings. Nick and Mae are fraternal twins. A fourth sibling named Franklin doesn't live in the area. Mae is married to Leo, Abby is married to David, and well, you know Nick was married to Anna. They were divorced three years ago," Randy told her.

"Now that you have the scoop on her family members, can you go and question them?"

"That's what Detective Hart is working on right now. We're questioning the Scott siblings and their spouses. It's been very challenging finding this crew. Someone knows something. It's important we speak with Jason since we know he and Tina had direct communication on the day of Anna's death. So, you haven't spoken to Jason?"

"No, I haven't met Jason. I didn't know how he was connected to any of this until just now. He must have gotten a new phone though."

"Darn," Randy said, "well it was worth a try. Did you see anything on it while you were snooping through it?"

"You mean researching and collecting evidence?" Kelsey said with a sly smile. "Jason's phone showed that one of his last locations was Fox Fitness. He's not a member of the gym."

"Interesting. Do you think he could be the kidnapper?"

"There was a photo of him in his phone and there is no way he was the kidnapper. He didn't have a mole," Kelsey said.

"Did you get a good look at the woman at the house? What was she doing?" he asked.

Kelsey told her dad the little that she and Justin heard that night including the banging and stomping.

"This family has secrets, Kelsey. Her uncle has a criminal past. I wouldn't be surprised if they have a connection to an organized crime group. These are things even the police don't want to get mixed up in. Let us take it from here, okay?" Randy said in a stern voice.

Kelsey reluctantly nodded.

"I mean it, Kelsey. This family is not one you want to mess with."

***

"Hey, Saff, do you have a date after work tonight?" Kelsey asked. "Your hair and makeup look amazing."

"Thanks, Kels! I do." Saffron smiled and blushed. "I met this guy Steven when I was out with Tanya at The Pirate Ship last weekend and he asked me out to dinner. I'm hoping he's as good-looking as I remember. Melissa kept giving free shots she was concocting so now I'm rethinking it."

Kelsey laughed, "She has a habit of doing that. The last time I went she made this drink that was a cross between a purple hooter and a lemon drop. Tasty, but it made my head spin."

Sam walked over to the front desk accompanied by a petite Asian girl wearing trendy athletic workout clothes from head to toe and sporting a casual ponytail.

"Hey, Kelsey. I want you to meet someone. This is my girl-friend, Sam. Short for Samantha."

"It's so nice to meet you," Kelsey said, shaking Samantha's hand.

"It's nice to meet you too. I decided to come and meet the person who has been making my boyfriend stronger and giving him these sexy muscles. Oh, and you can call me Sammy. Most of my friends do. It makes it easier, especially since Sam and I are dating now."

Sam blushed. "She also wanted to know if she could join the gym and start doing some training with you."

"Of course! I would love that. This is Saffron, our gym manager. She can set you up on with membership and schedule you for an orientation with me."

"That sounds great!" said Sammy, following Saffron into the office.

"Here, walk with me while you wait for Sammy to sign up," Kelsey said to Sam.

Sam nodded and followed Kelsey onto the gym floor as she cleaned up the mess members had left.

"She seems so sweet, Sam. I'm excited you brought her in."

"Yeah, I know she's done stuff like Pilates and yoga, but I don't think she's ever done weight training," Sam said as he helped put a foam roller away. "Hey, so did you find anything good on the phone?"

"I did. And I think it might help to find Tina. I told my dad about how Justin and I broke into Tina's house and found Jason's phone. I went to lunch with him, and he asked me if I knew Jason, so they'd already connected him with Tina because of her call history. He asked me for the phone, but it's already been wiped clean."

"Your dad? Why would he want the phone?" asked Sam.

"Did I not mention that my dad's the Oakview chief of police?"

"What? Your dad is the chief? How did I not know this about you? That's so cool. So, you're the chief's kid!" He made with quote fingers as he said, "Chief's."

Kelsey laughed, "Yep. My dad always thought I would become an officer like him, but I'm much better off here training and doing fun stuff all day. At one point, I thought I might want to be an EMT, but I think my fate was sealed the minute I walked in that door over there. Fox is my home now."

"I never wanted to become a police officer, either. There were kids at school who wanted to be one, but not me. I'm not a super physical person. I love my computer work even if it means tight butt muscles."

Just then, Sammy walked over.

"Did you just say 'tight butt'?" she said and then giggled.

"Yes, we all know about Sam's tight butt muscles, don't we?" Kelsey said. Sammy and Kelsey laughed, and Sam blushed.

"Maybe you two shouldn't work out together. Hey Justin! Or Charlie!? Want a new client?" Sam said.

"Hey now, don't give my clients away to other trainers. I think Sammy and I will get along just fine," Kelsey said as Sammy smiled and nodded.

"That's the problem," Sam chuckled. "I think you two may get along too well."

"It was so nice to meet you, Kelsey. I have an appointment on your calendar for this coming Monday afternoon," Sammy said.

"I'm looking forward to it. We'll get you started on a strength training plan. Make sure you come dressed in workout gear and shoes, and bring a water bottle and towel. What you're wearing right now is perfect. We'll sit down to chat and then do a fitness assessment."

Sammy nodded, gave Kelsey a thumbs up, and then gave Sam a peck on the cheek, making him blush again.

"Wow, I don't think I've ever seen a Black guy blush," Kelsey said, a big grin on her face.

Sam laughed, "I guess there's a first for everything."

***

After finishing her afternoon sessions, Kelsey found Justin stuffing his face with fruit in the breakroom. She sat down next to him to catch him up on her conversation with her dad.

"Wow, what will happen if they can't get people to cooperate in the interview process? Can they make them come in?" Justin asked as Kelsey helped herself to a piece of watermelon.

"I don't know. I think the spouse or ex-spouse is always the number one suspect, which puts Mr. Scott in the hot seat. The first thing we need to look at is motive. Who would want Anna dead? And does Tina know something that would help put the killer away? Is that why she was kidnapped? We can't cross out the fact there may be more than one person behind all of this. We're not sure what the kidnapper's connection to Anna is or if it's even related. The sooner we find Tina, the better. We know she didn't want to go with the kidnapper, but from what he said, it also sounded like he was doing it for her own good."

"Yeah, it was more like she was being a stubborn little kid, and he was trying to help her. It didn't seem like he was trying to hurt her. It was scary because she was trying so hard to escape his grasp. But what if he was trying to save her from the killer?

Unpopular opinion, I know. But we can't rule that possibility out. Maybe they know something we don't," Justin said.

Chapter 17

Sunday, September 18, 2022

With its steep gabled roof, the Tudor-style house came into view, framed perfectly by the large oak tree in the front yard. A wave of familiarity and warmth washed over Kelsey as she pulled into her parents' driveway.

Stepping inside, she was greeted by the comforting aroma of home-cooked food. Her mother stood at the stove, a spatula in hand. Brian sat at the kitchen table, engrossed in a video game. His eyes were wide with excitement. He squirmed in his chair, his whole body moving from side to side.

"Hi, Mom. Hi, Bri. Hey, Bri, do you need the bathroom? Why are you squirming like that?"

"Oh, hi, sweetie. I didn't even hear you come in. Your dad will be right down," Joanna James said.

"Hi, Kels. I'm just playing this racing game, and it's uhh, uhh, aww man, I lost," Brian said as he put his game down and looked up. "What's up?" he says, his bright green eyes sparkling in the morning sun. "Is Justin with you?"

"Umm, nothing much. Just working and stuff. Nah, Justin didn't come with me today.

He's at home studying for some certification. How's school and football?"

"It's good."

"Brian, tell Kelsey about your game on Friday,"

"Oh yeah. I scored two touchdowns, and we won the game," he said.

"Even though the other team's defense was brutal," Joanna chimed in. "Brian was amazing. He's so fast. Your dad caught it on video."

"That's awesome, Bri. I can't wait to see it."

Brian James had been playing Pop-Warner football since he was seven years old. Fast as lightning, his coaches made him a wide receiver. He and Randy constantly worked on running routes and catching the ball.

"I'm so proud of you. I need to come see one of your games soon," Kelsey said.

Randy descended the stairs, greeted Kelsey and Brian, then walked over to Joanna and kissed her. He wrapped his arms around her and asked if she needed any help. Randy and Joanna were high school sweethearts and had the kind of relationship most people strive for.

"This French toast smells amazing, Mom. It smells different than normal. Did you add something besides vanilla and cinnamon?" Kelsey asked as she helped to plate the food.

"I did! Wow, you have a good nose, Kelsey! I added a little cardamom to the egg batter. They use it in many Indian dishes. I found a recipe for it online and thought it might be nice to try something different. I made it a couple of weekends ago and I think it's a keeper. Brian and your dad both seemed to like it."

Ding! Dong!

Randy went to open the door, "Hey, Josh! It's great to see you. Welcome."

Kelsey's eyes grew wide. *What? My dad invited the new officer to brunch?* A wave of nausea came over her as she looked down at what she was wearing—an old pair of worn leggings and a ratty Stanford sweatshirt. *Is it too late to leave out the back? What if I get something stuck in my teeth? What if I sneeze while I'm eating? What if I spill food down the front of my shirt?* On the bright side, at least she threw on some new makeup this morning.

"Kelsey. Kelsey! Earth to Kelsey!"

Kelsey looked up to see her dad standing in front of her.

"You remember Josh, don't you?"

"Uh, sure. Hi, again," Kelsey said as she gave him a weak smile.

"Hey, Kelsey. It's nice to see you. Your dad invited me over for brunch to meet your family. When he told me about your mom's amazing French toast, I couldn't pass up the invite."

"Okay everyone, let's sit down and eat. Who wants a mimosa?" Joanna called out.

Kelsey's hand immediately shot up. Before she could get up to help her mom with the drinks, her phone dinged. A text from Saffron appeared.

hey, do u want to go shopping with Charlie and me at Hilltop Mall today?

sure. when? I need new sneakers. at brunch with my family right now. omg my dad invited this hot cop named Josh. I'm freaking out.

oooh. I want the scoop. 3 so you have plenty of time. pick up or meet there?

meet there

Nordy's bottom lot?

sounds good

The family gathered around the table for brunch, the delicious aroma of freshly cooked food filling the air. Randy, ever curious, focused on Josh, bombarding him with a barrage of questions. Josh, between bites, shared that he was born in Oakview but that he moved with his adoptive family to Seattle when he was three. He had a younger sister named Chelsea who lived with their parents in Seattle.

"Randy, stop interrogating the poor guy and let him eat!" Joanna finally said.

"When are you planning to check out Kelsey's gym, Josh?" Randy asked.

"Dad!" "Randy!" Joanna and Kelsey said in unison.

"What? It's an honest question."

"I've been meaning to get over there. I'd love to come by sometime this week. I don't want to be getting soft, you know?" Josh said, poking his abs.

"Sure, come in and check it out to see if it works for you. We have all the equipment anyone needs for a great workout. If you come in, I'll introduce you to our manager, Saffron. She can give you a tour of the place."

"Can't you do that, Kelsey?" Randy said.

"What? The tour?"

He nodded.

"I can. I mean, if you want me to. Saff does it so much better though because she gives tours fifty million times a day. I could do your tour though."

"That sounds great, Kelsey. I get off at seven most mornings so I could pop by any time after that."

"Sure, I can meet you at the gym at eight a.m. on Tuesday if that works for you. My client in that spot is out of town this week."

"That works for me. It's a date then. Eight on Tuesday. Thanks, Kelsey."

Chapter 18

Sunday, September 18, 2022

Saffron arrived at the mall first and waited for Kelsey and Charlie to arrive. At 3:05, the big, black Ford Raptor pulled into the lot, and Kelsey got out, walking over to Saffron's Mercedes.

"Hey, girl!" Saffron said, getting out of her car. "Okay, it's time to spill the tea!"

"Saff, it was so embarrassing. And guess what? I think my dad invited him over on purpose to set us up, and now I'm giving him a gym tour on Tuesday morning."

"Ooh, what time?"

"Eight."

"You'd better wake up early and put some makeup on that day. Speaking of makeup, yours looks nice."

"Thanks. I was experimenting this morning with a new BB cream and some blush and eyebrow makeup. How was your date with that guy Steven last night?"

"It was okay. I don't think he was my type. The whole time I listened to him brag about how long a fish he caught the last time he went out with his buddies and how he's exceptionally good at playing sports. I'm glad it was just for drinks because I don't think I would have lasted a whole dinner. But back to you. So, how hot is Josh?"

"Yikes. Sorry it didn't work out," Kelsey said. "Yeah, Josh is pretty hot. I think he's Italian. He's tall, and has dark hair and blue eyes. He's from Seattle, but he was born here."

"Ooh, a sexy Italian!" Saffron kidded.

Charlie pulled up and got out of her car. Charlie, short for Charlotte, had been training at Fox for nine years after leaving her hometown of Los Angeles right after high school. She was the tough one of the bunch—boot camp instructor meets Harley Quinn minus the pink hair.

"Hey, ladies! Sorry, I'm a little late. I had to call my mom back. She only calls when there's some kind of drama back home. It's part of the reason I left LA."

The trio walked through the mall, browsing store after store and making a few purchases here and there. Charlie and Kelsey found some new sneakers, and Saffron browsed through racks of athletic wear before selecting a stylish new workout shirt.

"Where to next, ladies?" Saffron asked.

"Can we go to Cabela's? I need to buy a gift card for my dad's birthday," said Charlie.

Kelsey and Saffron looked around at Cabela's while Charlie picked out a gift card from the rack in front. The store had so many cool items and Kelsey and Saffron tried on sunglasses while they waited for Charlie. They were just about to join her at the register when Kelsey saw a man wearing a white T-shirt, jeans, and white sneakers. He wore a baseball cap, but something about him caught Kelsey's eye. Then she saw it. The mole. *Could this be the man who kidnapped Tina? How many people have a mole there on the side of their face?* He stood two people behind Charlie. Kelsey grabbed Saffron and pulled her behind a display of jackets.

"I think that's Tina's kidnapper," Kelsey whispered. Taking her phone out, she took a few photos of the man. They stealthily made their way out the front door, and when Charlie exited, they pulled her into a neighboring store.

They watched the man exit the mall and then followed him, leaving plenty of distance between them so he wouldn't suspect anything. He got into a late-model Ford Explorer a few rows over from Chuckie. The trio climbed into Chuckie and Kelsey started the ignition.

"Okay if we go on a little adventure?" Kelsey asked as they pulled out of the lot several yards behind the man. "I'm sorry I dragged you guys into this, but I think this is our chance to find out where Tina is."

Saffron and Charlie both nodded and Saffron said, "We want to find Tina, too. It's amazing you spotted this guy, Kels."

Eventually, they ended up in a residential neighborhood and saw the man pull into the driveway of a gray house. Kelsey looked at the street sign.

"This is the Crenshaw house. Stafford Street. That was the street listed in Jason's phone for his parents," Kelsey said. *Did her own family kidnap her? Maybe Justin wasn't so far off when he said the person was trying to protect Tina, not hurt her.*

After watching the house for several minutes, the front door opened. The man climbed back into his Explorer with a younger guy. Kelsey identified the younger guy from the pictures on his phone. It was Jason Crenshaw. Leaving a good distance between Chuckie and the Crenshaws, Kelsey followed them into a Jack in the Box parking lot. The Crenshaws pulled into the short line at the drive-through, and Kelsey parked her truck in the lot near the drive-through exit.

"Jack in the Box?" said Charlie.

"Interesting. Jack in the Box tacos are one of Tina's favorite guilty pleasures. They might be leading us straight to her," Kelsey said.

Traffic was busy on the weekends on El Camino. Kelsey did her best to follow them without being caught. Eventually, the SUV pulled into the driveway of a large brick house framed by a picturesque green lawn with little rose bushes lining the front window. Kelsey pulled Chuckie around the corner and parked next to a public park.

"My dad said her AirPods pinged to this neighborhood. That house must be where they're keeping Tina."

"Let's walk around the block and see if we can see anything. Maybe we can look in the mailbox for something with the owner's name on it," Charlie said, taking charge.

"I should call Justin to let him know where we are," Kelsey said, suddenly unsure about the mission.

"Let's get closer to the house and text him the address. If we get kidnapped, he'll know where we are," said Saffron.

The daylight started to fade, which helped to camouflage them as they moved forward. The porch lights turned on. Kelsey took a picture of the house and the SUV and sent it to Justin. She also texted him the address and the descriptions of

Jason and his dad. He texted her back with *Are you crazy? Get out of there.*

Crouching behind some bushes next to the house across the street, which seemed empty, Kelsey, Saffron, and Charlie felt like sitting ducks. There was nothing to do but wait. Their attention was so laser-focused on the house they failed to notice a light turning on in the home they were hiding beside.

"Excuse me, what are you ladies doing in my bushes?" a voice said from behind them.

Chapter 19

Sunday, September 18, 2022

The three of them jumped. Kelsey could feel the tips of her ears get hot as she realized they had been caught. They turned around to see an older man in his late sixties or early seventies standing with his hands on his hips. He was wearing a red and green flannel button-down and blue jeans and looked a lot like Dick Van Dyke. His eyes were kind although he looked weary of the three young women in his yard.

"Umm, hi, sir. We were looking for our friend," said Charlie.

"In my bushes?"

"Well, no, we think our friend is in that house over there, and we wanted to surprise her for her birthday."

"Who is your friend? That's the Scott's house over there. It's just an older couple, and sometimes their adult kids stop by. They're all older than you three, though. Are you sure you have the right house? Who did you say you were looking for?"

"Did you say the Scotts' house?" Kelsey said.

"Yeah, great folks. Very friendly and family oriented. Hmm, come to think of it, there is the one grandson who stops by occasionally."

"I'm sorry we were in your bushes. We must have the wrong house," said Saffron.

He looked at all three of them, still a bit skeptical, however, he seemed to accept their apology and nodded. Thanking the man, Kelsey, Saffron, and Charlie quickly walked back toward Chuckie.

"What was that?" an out-of-breath Saffron said.

"I was so scared. I thought I was going to pee my pants," Kelsey said.

"Let's get the hell out of here," Charlie said.

"That must be her grandparents' house because no one besides Tina and her dad has the last name Scott. The sisters are both married. And the fourth sibling doesn't live near here," Kelsey said once they were back on the road. "They must be keeping Tina there. I don't know why the police haven't staked out this house yet. I feel like they're not even trying. This is so frustrating."

"They could also be keeping her at the house where he picked Jason up. Just because they're here doesn't mean Tina is. Or they could be moving her from location to location so no one can find her," said Charlie.

"The Jack in the Box food run is a dead giveaway. Tina loves their tacos. Plus, this is the neighborhood her AirPods pinged to. Ladies, I think we've just found Tina," Kelsey said, sure of herself.

Chapter 20

Sunday, September 18, 2022

Randy James sat staring at the screen saver on his computer. "What a mess," he mumbled, shaking his head. "What a goddamn mess." The sound of his cell phone pulled him out of his trance, and he looked at the Caller ID. Kelsey.

"Hi, hon. What's up?" he answered, sounding tired and deflated.

"David Crenshaw kidnapped Tina. I saw a guy at the mall with the same mole on the side of his face, so I followed him. He picked Jason up from the Crenshaw house and went to Jack in the Box. Then, they went to a house in the Aragon district. Why didn't you tell me Tina's grandparents lived in that area?" Kelsey said.

"We have an undercover staking the house out, but there hasn't been any sign of Tina," Randy said. "You need to be careful, Kelsey. We can't let the family know we're on to them."

"What else is Hart doing to work the case? Has he interviewed Jason?"

"Don't worry about it. Just keep yourself out of trouble. Hart is working on it. Promise me you'll take a step back. For Tina's sake. I've got to go, honey. I'll talk to you later," Randy said, hanging up.

Chapter 21

Monday, September 19, 2022

"I can't believe you did that without me!" Justin said, a little bit mad, and hurt at the same time. "You could have gotten yourself into some serious trouble! There's a murderer on the loose, Kelsey!"

"I know, I know. We didn't know what to do. The guy was right there at the mall, and we knew that if we followed him, he could lead us to Tina. What if we had found her?"

"But not at the expense of your safety. I don't want anything happening to you, or to Saffron or Charlie, for that matter."

"You're right. It was stupid. Sorry, Jus. It won't happen again. Promise."

"Okay, then. I'm gonna hold you to it."

"Not to change the subject, but are we hanging out at your place after work today?" Kelsey asked Justin.

"Yeah, I was thinking loaded baked potatoes with some grilled chicken. Sound good?"

Kelsey's eyes lit up as her head filled with visions of potato doused in crispy bacon pieces, green onion, little pieces of broccoli, and roasted red peppers.

"I'll take that drool running down your chin as a yes," Justin said as he walked away laughing.

***

Kelsey and Justin flopped down on the couch with their dinner plates. Justin turned on an old episode of CSI, and they zoned out. Kelsey picked through her potato which was smothered in bacon, chives, and grilled chicken. Justin mindlessly scooped his potato into his mouth.

After watching two episodes of CSI, Justin looked over to see Kelsey snoring on his couch. He placed a light blanket over her and quietly picked up the dinner plates and utensils, taking them into the kitchen. Turning on his computer in his bedroom, Justin started a new chapter in his continuing education class, "Kettlebell for Strength."

An hour later, he checked on Kelsey who was still asleep and starting to drool. Walking over to her, he flicked her ear gently. She startled and laughed, embarrassed she had fallen asleep. Wiping the drool from the corner of her mouth, Kelsey looked at her phone.

"Wow, it's ten-thirty already?" she said.

"You were out. I wasn't sure if you wanted to stay the night or head home," Justin said.

"Thanks for waking me. I think I'll head home. I'm sure Finley is wondering where I am."

As she stood up to leave, she grabbed her phone and bag and saw that she had an unread text. She gasped as she opened the message, *JUST MIND YOUR OWN BUSINESS.*

Chapter 22

Tuesday, September 20, 2022

J osh DeLuca pulled into the gym parking lot and glanced at his car's clock. It was 7:50 a.m. He was a few minutes early, so he checked his work email. An APB from a few days ago about Tina's kidnapping caught his eye. He considered asking Randy for more details and whether Hart could use additional help on the case, but ultimately decided against it. Sighing, he grabbed his gym bag and headed toward the front office.

"Hi, I'm here to meet Kelsey for an eight o'clock tour," he said to the young woman at the front desk.

"Hi, I'm Saffron, the gym manager. You must be Josh. Kelsey should be here any minute," Saffron said, standing up to shake Josh's hand. "You can take a seat if you'd like," she said pointing to the office chairs.

Hot cop is here. Hurry your butt up, Saffron texted Kelsey.

As Kelsey gave Josh the tour, he listened attentively and nodded to show he understood the workings of Fox Fitness. "You scan your card at the door, head to the locker room, and stow your belongings in a locker," she explained.

The tour itself was straightforward. Starting at the front of the gym, they walked past two rows of cardio machines. Moving on, Kelsey pointed out the various strength machines and equipment, including dumbbells and barbells. Finally, a spacious floor space was designated for mat work and stretching, where several people were already engaged in their routines.

"So, how long have you been a trainer here?" he asked.

"I've been training here for seven years, but I was a member before I started training. I've always enjoyed working out. Before joining this gym as a member, I mainly worked out at my parents' home gym. My last job as a work-at-home telemarketer was horrible, so I decided to get a membership here to blow off some steam and get away from the monotony of staying at home all day. I ended up loving it here. Then, Saffron suggested I become a trainer because I was always here."

"I agree. There's something different about going to an actual gym and having other people working out around you. The gym environment seems great here," he said as he looked around again.

"I know exactly what you mean."

"Great, so should I go up front to sign up with your friend?"

"Yes, I'll go up there with you. I'm meeting my nine o'clock client next, so I have a few minutes."

Saffron looked up from playing with Finley and said, "Done so soon?"

"Josh knows his way around a gym, so I just showed him where stuff was. It's not like the gym is that big, Saff."

"True. Okay, Josh. Ready to join?"

"I am. Just tell me where to sign."

Chapter 23

Tuesday, September 20, 2022

*H*ey, I hope you don't mind. I asked Saffron for your number. Would you like to go out for dinner, a drink, or both? I'm off work today. This is Josh, by the way.

Kelsey felt her heart drop to her stomach. *He wants to go on a date? With ME?*

She walked across the gym floor and over to Justin, "Hey, something's come up. Raincheck on tonight?"

"Sure. Everything okay?"

"Yeah, I'll tell you tomorrow."

"Alrighty then."

Sure! Dinner and drinks sound good. Did you have a place in mind?

I was hoping you'd pick the place since I'm new here. Is that okay?

Sure! How about The Pig and Whistle Pub on 25th Avenue? They have fantastic food and a full bar. Does 8 work?

That works. Should I pick you up at your place?

Let's meet there.
OK, see you then.

***

Kelsey slid into a pair of black jeans, a black tank top, and a sheer floral-print blouse she recently purchased. A little makeup, and voilà. Giving Finley a little kiss goodbye, she grabbed her purse, phone, and keys. Then she took a deep breath.

With five minutes to spare, Kelsey pulled into the Pig and Whistle parking lot. Josh's black Chevy Camaro pulled into the spot next to her.

"Wow! That is one impressive truck!" he said, whistling at Chuckie.

"Yeah," Kelsey said, giving Chuckie a pat on the front hood. "I bought him last year. He's got the works—lift kit, twenty-twos, his matte black paint job, and a few other aftermarket goodies. I grew up going to monster truck rallies with my dad. People make fun of me because I'm short and I drive a big truck but I tell them it's like a big booster seat. I can see everything around me when driving."

"Good point! I never thought of that. So, your dad likes monster trucks, huh?"

"You can ask him all about it. I'm sure he'll talk your ear off. I was three years old the first time he took me. Earmuffs and all."

"I love it. You and your dad seem close."

"We are. Very," Kelsey said, thinking of her dad and smiling at the good childhood memories.

Josh held the door open for her, and they settled on a table in the back. The British-style pub had a long menu that included fish and chips, bangers and mash, and cottage pie. A young woman dressed in a black and white plaid shirt, jeans, and apron walked over, ready to take their order. "Welcome to Pig and Whistle! Our specials tonight are chicken schnitzel with fried green beans, and beef and ale pie. Oh, hey, Kelsey! How's it going?"

"Hi, Cass! I didn't know you worked here. It's good to see you," Kelsey said, recognizing her old classmate.

"It's good to see you, too! This is only my second week here, but I like it so far. This place has personality. I love all the cool memorabilia on the wall. Plus, the food and drinks are off the hook. What can I get you guys?"

"I'll have a glass of your house rosé and the shepherd's pie."

Josh's eyes scanned the menu. "I'll have a Sierra Nevada on tap and the fish and chips." He looked at Kelsey with a bit of sadness. "Fish always reminds me of home."

"Where are you from?" Cassandra chimed in.

"Seattle. I grew up there," he said, nervously sliding the salt-shaker from hand to hand.

"Isn't Seattle where they have that market where they throw the fish?" Cass continued.

Josh laughed and said, "Yeah, it is. There's a big fishing community up there."

"Cool," Cassandra said as she collected their menus. "I've always wanted to visit. I'll be right back with your drinks."

"That's the nice part about living in the area that you grew up in," Josh said after Cassandra left the table. "You see people around town that you know all the time. She seemed like a nice girl."

"We went to school together. We weren't in the same friend group but had a few classes together and got along well. Group projects and stuff, you know. Since you're new in town, I'd be happy to show you the best spots. We can even invite some of the gym people to hang out."

"Are your coworkers your main group of friends? Your dad mentioned that Justin is like a best friend to you."

"He is. We hang out a lot, just as friends. He moved here from Texas last year, and we bonded over our love of food. Some girl is going to get lucky one day because he is a mean chef. I don't think there's anything he can't make. Oh, and Saffron is my best girlfriend. We do girly stuff together, like shopping and sleepover movie nights."

"Very cool. So, do you take all the new guys in town and show them the ropes?" he asked, smirking.

"No, just you and Justin," Kelsey blushed.

The food arrived, and the rest of the night went off without a hitch. Kelsey and Josh found out they had some things in common. They both loved the beach, him spending his summers at Lake Sammamish State Park as a kid and Kelsey going on family summer trips to Lake Tahoe. They were both mystery novel fanatics and animal lovers. Josh told her about Shadow, his German shepherd, and how one day he would do a road trip to bring him back to the Bay Area.

The conversation turned to food, and Kelsey was excited when she found out Josh loved all types of food including international cuisines. According to Josh, the most interesting thing he had ever eaten was an Asian fruit called durian, known for being stinky. He told her he didn't care for it, and the smell was beyond bad.

They laughed as Josh told her stories about things that had happened while he was on the job—stories about people yelling and screaming at him, or throwing things at him and his partner. When they finished eating, Kelsey excused herself to use the restroom and passed Cass on the way. Cass leaned over and whispered, "Where'd you find *him*? What a catch!" Kelsey smiled back and nodded in agreement.

As Kelsey arrived back at the table, Josh stood up to help her with her coat as they prepared to leave the restaurant. The cold fall air made Kelsey shiver.

"We'd better get you back home before you turn into a popsicle. I had fun tonight, Kelsey. I'm glad we did this."

"I had fun, too," she told him. There was a short, uncomfortable silence and finally, Josh asked, "See you at the gym tomorrow?" as he helped Kelsey into Chuckie.

Kelsey nodded and started the engine, turning up the heat, and rubbing her hands together to warm them. Her phone vibrated in her purse.

"Dad?"

"Kelsey, honey, we have Tina. She's fine, but we're putting her in protective custody. I wanted to let you know she's okay, though. We gave her back her phone so you can text her. We haven't made a public statement, so please don't tell anyone except Justin. We're keeping this under wraps until we know more about how the kidnapping is related to Anna's murder."

A flood of relief filled Kelsey as she felt a tear run down her cheek. *Tina is okay.* She picked up the phone to call Justin.

Chapter 24

Wednesday, September 21, 2022

K elsey strolled into Fox Fitness, entering the familiar environment of clanging weights and whirring ellipticals. Knowing Tina was safe in police custody had taken a massive weight off her shoulders. The morning was a blur as Kelsey finished one training session after another. Even the complaining from her high-maintenance client, Jessica, didn't bring her spirits down.

At around 11:30, her stomach grumbled. Visions of a falafel-filled gyro danced around in her head. Known for their homemade falafel and hummus, Mykonos Kitchen was the best Mediterranean food in town. A medicine ball whizzed by her shoulder, snapping her out of her trance, and she looked up to see Justin laughing at her.

"Ready to go, Kelsey Sue?"

Kelsey stuck her tongue out at him and went to grab her bag and keys. He knew she hated it when he called her by her first and middle names in that thick cowboy drawl of his.

As Kelsey and Justin pulled up to the restaurant, she said, "Now that we know Tina is safe, I say we go find that Jason guy and make him tell us what he knows."

"We've got to do things carefully, though, Kels. I'm sure their family knows your dad is the chief of police."

"Kelsey? Excuse me. Are you Kelsey?" a young guy was running toward her. Kelsey was shocked to see it was Jason Crenshaw.

"Yeah, that's me."

"I'm Jason. Jason Crenshaw. You know my cousin, Tina. I need your help."

Chapter 25

Doing a double-take, Kelsey wondered, *Did I just manifest this guy?*

"I was going to come looking for you. How did you find me?" Kelsey said to Jason.

"I followed you from the gym because I didn't want to lose my nerve. I've been wanting to talk to you. My mom, dad, uncle, and aunt have been helping to hide Tina from her dad. But when I went to see her this morning, she was gone."

"You know the police are looking for you."

"I know. It was my dad's idea. We think Tina's dad killed her mom because of something he just found out. Something that could change Tina's life forever."

Kelsey nodded, waiting for him to continue.

"Tina and her mom, Anna, did some DNA ancestry tests for fun and got the results a few days before Anna died. They found out there was no way that my Uncle Nick could be Tina's dad. Anna cheated on my Uncle Nick early on in their relationship.

When she told him he went ballistic. Neither Anna nor Tina wanted to talk to him until he cooled down."

"That must have been what they argued about at the farmers' market," Kelsey said, turning to Justin, who nodded. "So you think Nick killed Anna because of this?"

"That's what my family thinks. Especially Leo. He was very protective over Anna and now Tina. We didn't want to take any chances. Someone killed Anna, and we don't know who it is for sure. Tina is so stubborn. My dad and I have been trying to convince her to stay out of sight until they find Nick. She swears her dad would never hurt her but he's got a temper. Plus, he's gone AWOL and isn't answering anyone's calls or texts. We wanted to keep Tina safe. Tina has been staying at our grandparents' house. I'm scared the minute she surfaces, her dad will try to hurt her. If he was mad enough to kill Anna, who knows what he'll do to Tina now that he knows he's not her real dad."

"But it's not her fault her mom cheated, and he's not her dad. Why would he punish Tina?" Kelsey asked.

"He and my Aunt Anna had a volatile relationship when they were together. For as long as I can remember, she drove him crazy. Nick went over to Anna's house the night of her murder, and they ended up arguing. He hit her and she called my Aunt Mae crying. My Uncle Leo was livid when he found out Nick hit Anna. He was ready to find Nick and tear him a new one. Leo has always been protective of Anna. Leo introduced Nick to Anna when Anna was in her teens, so he felt bad when their relationship went south. Nick must have gone back to Anna's later that night and killed her."

Things were making a lot more sense. Tina's own family kidnapped her to protect her, not hurt her.

"Why didn't you just call the police?"

"We have no proof that Nick killed Anna or that Tina is in danger," said Jason. "We would also get in trouble for kidnapping her, so we decided not to involve the police and just wait things out."

"Interesting," Justin said. "So, you thought it would make more sense to keep her locked in your grandparents' basement?"

"It wasn't like that. When Tina woke up, she was a lot calmer. We told her we would do anything to protect her. And that it was for her safety. What if she had been home when her mom's attacker was there?" he explained, his hands fidgeting nervously, "She started to understand the severity of the situation. She started crying because she said she didn't know who to trust. We didn't lock her up. She wasn't a prisoner. She could have left at any time. We convinced her to stay. At least for a couple of weeks. She promised.""Did your mom go to Anna's house looking for something?" Kelsey asked.

"You mean after Anna was killed?" Jason said, and she nodded. "My mom?" Jason said, confused. "Oh. That was my Aunt Mae. How do you know about that? She said something about Tina needing some personal items. I don't know, girl stuff or something. She said she would pick them up on the way home from work since it was on her way."

"She was looking for something. What was she looking for? And it wasn't just some personal items," Kelsey said, still suspicious of Jason and his motives.

Jason looked down sheepishly. "This is a little embarrassing. I went to Tina's house after we kidnapped her to grab a few things for her. I dropped my phone somewhere in her house. I don't know where. I must have been nervous to go into the house after the murder. I didn't realize I had lost my phone until I returned to my grandparents' house. My aunt went to the house to find my phone so I wouldn't become a suspect. My aunt said she tried calling it, but it didn't ring in the house. The phone must have been on silent."

"I went back to the house the next day to see if I could find it, but it wasn't in any of the places I had been in. I hope I don't end up being a suspect."

"So, why did you want to talk to me?" Kelsey asked, changing the subject.

"Tina told me you're the only person outside our family she can trust. I thought she might be with you at the gym or your place. She was scared, Kelsey. I think it hadn't sunk in yet that someone brutally killed her mom, you know? We kept reminding her that there was a killer out there, and we didn't know who it was or why the person killed her mom. She told me you've always been there for her and that you're the one person she knows she can trust. Tina and I were close when we were little kids. We started hanging out again after reconnecting at a family gathering a few weeks ago. I need your help to find her."

"Okay ..." Kelsey said, extremely confused. "So back up. You went to the house where your family was keeping her, your grandparents' house, and she wasn't there?"

He sighed, and a small tear formed at the corner of his eye. "Yeah, she wasn't there."

"Did you ask your grandparents what happened?" she asked him.

"They went out of town yesterday morning, so they weren't at the house. That's why I went to check on Tina. I knew she was alone. Someone must have been scoping out the house, and when they saw no one was home, they went in and kidnapped her. I'm scared it was her dad. We told her to keep the door locked, but if it was her dad, she might've opened the door for him."

"How do you know she didn't just leave?" Justin asked.

"I guess you're right. But do you think Tina left? And where would she go?"

"Besides me, who else would Tina trust?" Kelsey asked, digging for information to find out who Tina and her mom were closest to in the family.

"Tina has always been close to my Uncle Leo, mainly because Uncle Leo is like a big brother to Anna," Jason said.

"And you've asked him if he's seen her?" Kelsey asked.

"He said he hasn't. He's looking for her, too," Jason said.

The three exchanged information and agreed to update each other on any developments regarding Tina. Jason shook Kelsey and Justin's hands, thanking them.

***

"Well, what do you think?"

"I think he sounds like he's telling the truth. He seemed like a nice fella and all. Since Leo was so close to Anna, I wonder if he knows more than he's telling everyone," Justin said, "I still don't think we can fully trust this Jason guy though. He was part of the kidnapping after all."

"A nice fella? Is that what you said?" Kelsey says to Justin, making fun of his cowboy accent.

"Hardee har har, you think you're so funny, Miss Kelsey Sue," he replied jokingly. "Your place tonight for a brainstorming session? I can see your brain movin' in your head it's so full."

Chapter 26

Wednesday, September 21, 2022

After finishing a leg workout, Kelsey and Justin were starving. After work, they placed a to-go order from Brawn's Steakhouse—ribeye and garlic mashed potato entrées with spring veggies. After picking up the food, they pulled up to Kelsey's condo. Randy was sitting in his car waiting for them.

"Hi, Kels. Hey, Justin," Randy said, opening his car door.

"Hi, Dad, why are you here? What's up?"

"Hi, Mr. James, we were just going to have dinner. We ordered plenty of food. Your daughter eats a lot. Would you like to join us?" Justin said as Kelsey elbowed him.

"Thanks, Justin. No, this will only take a few minutes. I wanted to catch you and talk to you about something important," Randy said, with a serious look on his face.

Finley ran to greet them as they entered the condo. Taking Fin's leash off the hook, Justin headed outside with the pup to give Randy and Kelsey some privacy. Leaning forward in his chair and pressing his fingers together with his elbows on his knees, Kelsey felt a pang in her side. She knew this look. It was the "I need to talk to you about something very serious, Kelsey" pose. She grabbed the edge of the couch cushion with sweaty palms.

"I need to talk to you about something, Kelsey. As you know, Tina is in our care. She's not in trouble. She's in a very safe place. She is working with the police and wants to find out who killed her mom. We have some evidence pointing to Nick Scott. We think his motive has to do with the fact he found out that Tina is not his biological daughter."

"Okay ..." Kelsey said. "What's wrong, Dad? You're sweating. Are you sick? Do I need to call an ambulance?"

Randy continued, "No, no, just listen." He paused for a second and Kelsey's stomach made a loud gurgling sound. She wrapped her arms around herself to stanch the noise.

"What's going on, Dad? What do you have to tell me? You're scaring me."

"Twenty-four years ago, I made a mistake. It was a horrible mistake, and I felt bad while it was happening. I felt so guilty even when it was over. I had an affair with a married woman."

Kelsey's eyes opened wide. "What are you saying?"

He continued, "This was a long time ago, remember. I thought it was behind me. This woman and I had both moved on with our lives."

"What affair are you talking about? You and Mom have been together forever. You love each other. Does Mom know about this? Why are you telling me this?"

"Okay, okay, calm down, Kels. Telling you this is harder for me than you know."

"Calm down? It's hard for YOU? You just come over and drop this random bomb on me and think that I'm going to be calm about it?"

"I know. I'm sorry. But this is important. Yes, your mom knows about the affair. I told her years ago after I ended it with the woman," he continued.

"So, who was it? Is it someone I know? Is it someone Mom knows?" The questions poured out like hot volcanic lava.

"Yes. I mean, yes, you know her. Let me finish. I didn't know that the woman I was seeing had gotten pregnant. And she had a little girl. Just recently she found out her daughter is not her husband's, or rather ex-husband's," he said. "Kelsey, the woman was Anna."

Just then, Justin shuffled back in with Finley, and Kelsey stood up, hyperventilating, her arms and legs tingling. Justin rushed over, put his hands on her shoulders, and guided her back down on the couch.

"Kels, what happened? What's going on?" Justin looked over at Randy. "What did you tell her? Why is she freaking out like this?"

Even Finley was a bit uneasy and hopped up on the couch next to Kelsey, whimpering. Kelsey closed her eyes to stop the room from spinning. Opening them slowly, she started to gather her thoughts, and her dad and Justin stared at her. Finally, Kelsey took a deep breath and started talking.

"My dad had an affair with Anna. Tina is his daughter." The tears came pouring down Kelsey's cheeks, and with it, a flood of emotions. Justin was in shock as well.

"That means ... Tina's your sister?" Justin said, putting the details together.

Randy continued, "Anna came to me about a week and a half ago and told me her daughter must be mine and not Nick's. She said the DNA test showed Tina had no relation to Nick. I was just as surprised as you are now. I asked her if she was sure Tina was mine and not someone else's. She said yes and that I was the only person she had been with besides Nick at that time. I'm so sorry, Kels. I've always loved your mother. And you. And Brian. I never wanted to give my family up. I realized I didn't want to be with Anna."

"Does Mom know?" Kelsey said, her heart still thumping out of her chest.

"She knows now. It was killing me not telling her. I held on to it for three days after Anna told me, not knowing what to do or how this would change our family. I knew I had to come clean. Like I said, she already knew about the affair I had with Anna all those years ago. But telling her that I had a daughter with the woman I had an affair with was even more difficult than telling her about the affair itself. Anna was killed a few days after she told me. Justin, I'm sorry for bringing you into our family drama. I know this one's on me. I guess this really makes you part of the family."

"Well, Mr. J, I just can't help but wonder how we can help. Is there evidence that will prove that Mr. Scott is the one who killed Mrs. Scott?"

"Good question, Justin. I can't give exact details. But yes, if we catch Nick, we feel that we have evidence that he was the one who killed Anna. Whether there is enough evidence is the question. The problem is, we can't find him."

"As far as Tina goes, we figured out she was being held at her grandparents' house. One of our informants stayed in a vacant property across the street. There wasn't anyone except family members. And you, Saffron, and Charlie, of course. Tina walked into the station last night. If she hadn't, we would have gone in to extract her from the house."

"Does Tina know that you're her biological father?" Justin asked.

"She does now. I spoke to Tina after she came into the station. Anna was very nonchalant about it to Tina and told her that her biological father was long gone and out of the picture. She probably figured it would be better if Tina just went on living her life with Nick as her dad."

Chapter 27

Thursday, September 22, 2022

Kelsey was ecstatic as she looked at her training schedule for the day. Sam, Sylvia, Caroline, Sarita, Karl, Danny, and Jennifer were solid clients who worked hard and showed up. Sylvia brought Kelsey chocolate chip cookie dough protein bites with protein powder mixed into the batter, and Justin had finished them off before Kelsey noticed.

"Justin! Where are all the cookie bites Sylvia made for me?" Kelsey yelled across the gym.

"Oops," said Justin, walking away to train his next client.

"Hey, Kels, do you want to get food with Charlie and me?" asked Saffron.

"Yes, please. Where are we going?"

"We were thinking of going over to the taco truck."

"Sounds good to me. Justin, you want me to bring you back something?"

"The usual, please," Justin said, smiling, his stomach growling. "And sorry about the protein bites. They were so tasty. Tell

Sylvia if she makes you more to make me some, too. I'll pay her for them."

Kelsey, Saffron, and Charlie arrived at the taco truck and stood in line. The scent of Mexican spices and chiles filled the air, and Kelsey's stomach growled.

"Suresh and I plan to play pickleball this Saturday at Hudson Park. We reserved the court from two to four p.m. Do you guys want to come? Maybe Justin would like to join as well?" Charlie asked Saffron and Kelsey.

"I'm in," Kelsey said, "I'll ask Justin. He's usually off early on Saturdays like I am, but I don't know if he made plans for the afternoon.

"Yeah, I can make it too," said Saffron. "I'm working until noon."

"Great! I'll let Suresh know. I'm sure you guys will like him. He's high energy, like me, but not obnoxious. There's a fine line," Charlie said, and Saffron and Kelsey laughed.

Kelsey, Saffron, and Charlie returned to the gym and brought the food into the break room. Kelsey had two spicy carne asada tacos and two spicy chicken tacos; Saffron, her usual vegetarian burrito with a side of guacamole and pico de gallo; and Charlie, a super burrito with carnitas minus the sour cream and rice. Justin joined them a half hour later, sitting down to devour his usual four carne asada street tacos, extra spicy, with a side of guac and chips. He looked ravenous as he sat down and dug in.

Kelsey's phone buzzed. It was a text from Randy.

Kelsey, can you meet Detective Hart and me at the station later today? Bring Justin if he wants to help. We have a plan.

Chapter 28

Thursday, September 22, 2022

T he pitter-patter of the rain outside turned into heavier rainfall, followed by thunderstorms. Oakview's fall weather was always unpredictable. One day, it was sunshine, the next, rain and wind. The gym was nearly empty as Kelsey and Justin rearranged the equipment. Kelsey became teary-eyed as she rolled Joe over with the other barbells, patting it, and said, "It's okay. She'll be back."

"Talking to inanimate objects again, Kels?" Justin said from behind her. Kelsey jumped, then slugged Justin on the shoulder.

"Ouch! It's a good thing today wasn't shoulder day," Justin joked.

"You scared me! But okay, you caught me," Kelsey said, a tear slipping down her cheek as she thought about Tina again.

"Aww, Kels." Justin reached for a hug and Kelsey started crying into his shirt.

"I just miss her, you know. I haven't seen her since finding out she's my sister." Kelsey stood to wipe her tears with the back of her sweatshirt and looked up at Justin.

"I know. But Tina's safe now, and you'll be able to see her again soon. You can text her, right? Didn't your dad say she has her phone back?" Justin said sympathetically.

Kelsey nodded, "We've been texting a lot. I miss seeing her in person, though. I wish everything could go back to normal."

"I know. And this is why we're helping the police. To try and solve this case," Justin said, walking over to the hanging yellow and black straps. "Here, help me untangle this TRX. I don't know what people do to these things to get them all caught up like this."

"What do you think the plan could be?" asked Kelsey as she flipped the straps over and under to fix them.

"I'm sure the goal is to get Tina's dad out of hiding. They sound like they have some good evidence against him."

"True. I can't imagine what the evidence could be other than the murder weapon," Kelsey said.

"I wonder who else knows about your dad being Tina's dad? So far, it's me, you, and your mom. Does Brian know? What about the other officers in the department?" Justin asked.

Kelsey pulled her phone out and called her dad. Randy picked up his office phone right away.

"Randy James."

"Hi, Dad, I'm not on speaker, right?"

Hi, Kelsey! Are you on your way? No, you're not on speaker. I'm in my office with the door closed. Is there something you wanted to tell me?"

"Justin and I are about to leave Fox. Who else knows you're Tina's dad?

He paused for a minute. "I haven't formally announced it, but it's been recorded in the police reports for Tina's kidnapping and Anna's murder so Hart and anyone else who pulls up the file would know. The only reason I'm so heavily involved is because Oakview doesn't see very many homicides or kidnappings."

"Got it. Okay, that's all I wanted to ask. See you in a few."

Kelsey and Justin arrived at the police station and buzzed in at the front intercom. Moving past a row of desks on one side and a wall of filing cabinets on the other, they saw Randy sitting at his desk and Detective Hart standing in the doorway.

Randy led them down the hallway to the small conference room with a table, chairs, projector, and landline phone. He opened the files on the table and neatly spread their contents out for Kelsey and Justin to see. After swearing both to secrecy, Randy briefed them.

"We believe that Nick Scott is working from his boss's house in Redwood Shores. We don't have proof, but we've been surveilling his boss, Dalton Brooks. The patterns Brooks has displayed lead us to believe he is hiding Nick. We've tried knocking on Brooks's door, but there's no answer. We haven't seen Nick leave or arrive at Brooks's house, so we have no precedence for a warrant. We don't know their next move, but we have eyes on the condo. Nick and Anna finalized their divorce three years ago after a two-year separation. There was some domestic violence during the relationship, but the police were never called on any of the instances. Nick's admin says she hasn't heard from him, but Dalton told her he was working remotely on a special project. Hart spoke to Dalton in person at the office, and Dalton confirmed what the admin said about Nick working remotely. He claimed not to know where Nick was but that he would pass on our message the next time Nick checked in with him. We obtained a warrant to search Nick's apartment and vehicle. His apartment yielded traces of Anna's blood in the bathroom sink once we did a luminol test. The small amount of blood isn't enough for a conviction, but it's the only lead we have right now, so that's what we're following. Plus, he has a motive. We couldn't find his car, so we didn't have a chance to search it. Currently, we have an APB out on him. Unfortunately, we still have not found the murder weapon and can't find a motive for anyone else to have wanted to hurt or kill Anna."

"Is Mr. Scott left-handed?" Kelsey asked.

"I'm not sure what hand Mr. Scott writes with."

"I'm just asking because Tina said that her mom's head was hit on the right side of her face. Is that what the coroner came up with?"

Randy opened the file. "Yes, that's correct. Kelsey, you're right. Smart girl. The murderer was probably left-handed."

"Exactly. And if I'm correct, there are fewer left-handed people than right-handed ones."

Randy looked up at Detective Hart, who nodded.

"I've been paying attention to that during the interviews, sir," Hart said. "So far, none of the family members have used their left hand to write. I'm not finished with the interviews yet so that doesn't mean it's not one of them. Only Abby, David, and Jason have come forward."

"Do we think there is anyone else related to Anna or Tina who is in trouble? Do you think Nick could be in trouble?" Justin asked.

"Not at this time. But we have very little information to go off. Tina is willing to help us find her dad, especially if it means clearing his name. We can ask her what hand he writes with."

Randy continued, "The plan involves using Tina to draw Nick out of hiding. While we do not believe he poses a direct threat to her, we will ensure she has constant heavy protection. The one place that Nick knows Tina loves is the gym, which is why we selected Fox for this operation. Undercover agents will be present tomorrow night posing as gym members while you train Tina."

Kelsey felt a lump in her throat. She was right. They were using her sister as bait.

Chapter 29

Friday, September 23, 2022

The five o'clock spin class let out and the sweaty members shuffled into the locker room. The class instructor, Sally, swung her bag over her shoulder and went into the breakroom to grab her lunch tote. Kelsey and Justin sat at the table sharing a plate of nachos from the taco truck, and Sally said, "You two are always here. Do you ever go home?"

Kelsey chuckled and said, "It doesn't feel like it."

As the hum of the gym started to settle down and members left for the day, Justin said, "I'm kind of nervous about this. How 'bout you?"

"I'm so nervous. I swear if Mr. Scott comes in and tries to kidnap her, I'm going to pounce on him. I can't believe my dad would take a risk like this," Kelsey said, bunching up her fists in anger.

"Kels, I don't think they have any other options. It sounds like everything is a dead end other than the blood on the sink."

Tina would text Nick, asking him to meet her at the gym at seven p.m. If they got lucky, Nick would show up. The setup looked like this:

Undercover One and Undercover Two would walk in together as a couple.

Undercover Three would come in a few minutes later.

Undercover One would sweep the gym, women's restroom, and locker room. She would then do a five-minute warm-up on the elliptical, keeping an eye out for suspicious behavior at the front door. She would head over to the weight section, where she would lift some light weights.

Undercover Two would do a similar routine. He would sweep the male restroom and locker room and meet Undercover One for her warm-up and strength workouts. He would be mic'd up so Randy and the rest of the team could hear him.

Undercover Three would have a session with Justin. He would also be mic'd up.

Tina would walk in with Undercover Four, a woman named Jill who looked like she was in her early twenties but who was really in her mid-thirties. They would have a session with Kelsey.

Undercovers Five and Six would be by the front door, having a conversation. They would enter behind Tina and Jill.

Undercover Seven would stand by the men's locker room near the back emergency exit, pretending to be on the phone the whole time.

With this setup, all entrances and exits would be covered, and Tina would remain in the middle of the gym, surrounded by Jill, Kelsey, Justin, and Undercover Three.

Everyone took their places, aware of their surroundings and the front door. Tina looked over at Kelsey and smiled. Kelsey's heart melted, and she smiled and nodded at Tina, trying to hold back the tears. From the front window of the gym, Undercovers Five and Six saw a man wearing dark-rimmed glasses, jeans, and a flannel sherpa jacket. It wasn't Tina's dad, but he looked suspicious. The man started pacing in front of the gym, making a call on his cell phone. But then, he walked over to a late-model vehicle and drove away. False alarm. Fifteen more minutes went by.

Twenty. Thirty. Nothing. At this point, Jill and Tina had completed over 100 bodyweight squats.

The agents rotated positions according to plan. Officer Two came over to Jill, Tina, and Kelsey and quietly told them they needed to let Tina be by herself and to stay nearby. The plan was to make her seem more approachable as if no one was paying attention to her. Randy messaged Jill that Tina should text her dad again, asking if he was on his way. With Undercovers One and Two on the ellipticals (these were the easiest cardio machines to jump off), Kelsey and Justin cleaning up the gym and walking around, Undercover Three stationed by the back door, the two front door officers at the stretching area still talking, and Jill and Officer Five starting up a conversation near the front of the gym (not as far out as the two front door officers were), Tina climbed onto a spin bike, the most challenging piece of cardio equipment to pull someone off. If Nick was stupid enough to try and kidnap her himself, he wouldn't be able to grab her fast enough, and officers would arrest him.

Two more hours passed. Mr. Scott was a no-show. The mission was aborted. Jill, Tina, and Kelsey headed to the locker rooms and moved to the emergency exit where Undercover Three was waiting. Undercovers One and Two left through the front door, and Justin headed back toward the men's locker room. Kelsey opened the back door where the unmarked police car driven by Detective Hart waited. Tina and Jill climbed into the car, and Hart drove off. A Honda Civic with Undercovers One and Two followed them. The other officers left one by one through the gym's front door. Justin and Kelsey were the only ones left. Kelsey's phone rang. It was Randy.

"Hey, Dad, I'm putting you on speaker. Justin and I are the only ones left here at the gym."

"Hey, Kels. I'm sorry this didn't work out. You guys did a great job. I thought for sure this would have brought Nick out of hiding. I guess we're onto Plan B. The team will get started on that tomorrow. Two officers are sitting in the parking lot in separate cars out front, ready to escort you back home. I love you, Kelsey. Stay alert like I taught you, okay, honey? You too, Justin. You're a big guy but can never be too safe."

"Will do, Mr. J," said Justin.

"Thanks, Dad. Love you too. I'll talk to you tomorrow, okay?"

"Are you coming over to my place?" Kelsey asked Justin. He nodded and told the two officers that only one needed to escort them back to Kelsey's.

Once they had parked, Kelsey and Justin waved to the escorting officer.

As Kelsey unlocked her front door, a chill came over her. "Finley! Fin!" she called out. When Finley heard Kelsey approaching, he always came right to the door. Goosebumps rose on Kelsey's arms, and she reached out to grab Justin's arm. Where was Finley?

Chapter 30

Friday, September 23, 2022

Her heart pounded in her chest. Slowly pulling out her phone and pepper spray, Kelsey reached to turn the light on in the living room. A man was sitting on her couch. Kelsey did a double take. It was Nick Scott. Finley was fast asleep next to Mr. Scott, who seemed to be slowly dozing off himself.

"Mr. Scott?" Kelsey said slowly and tentatively. "What are you doing in my home?"

Nick Scott jerked his head up, suddenly aware of where he was, and blinked a few times.

"Hi, Kelsey. I'm sorry we're meeting again under these circumstances." His voice was soft and gentle. He rubbed his eyes and slowly stood up. Kelsey and Justin both took a step back. Mr. Scott raised his hands to show he wouldn't harm them. Finley stirred. Mr. Scott looked down at him and smiled. "Your dog is a sweetheart. He came right to me."

"I'm not sure what you're doing here, but I think you need to leave," Justin said, standing tall. Fin's head popped up, and he ran to Kelsey, hiding behind her.

"I need your help, Kelsey. It's not what anyone thinks. I'm running out of options. My life is falling apart because everyone thinks I murdered Anna. My own family doesn't trust me. Can I please have a few minutes of your time to explain?"

Justin and Kelsey looked at one another, and Justin shrugged. Mr. Scott seemed desperate, not angry or threatening.

"Okay, I'll listen to what you have to say—on one condition," Kelsey said.

"What's that?" Mr. Scott said skeptically.

"That you don't waste our time by lying to us. If you killed Anna, you need to turn yourself in. We're not going to help you hide a crime."

"Of course. I would never do that. I want my daughter back in my life and to have my name cleared," he said, then turned to Justin, "Sorry, we haven't met. I'm Nick Scott."

"Justin Reed," Justin said, shaking Mr. Scott's hand.

"I'm sorry to bring you guys into this. Please don't call the police. I'm at your mercy right now. I don't know who to turn to for help. Tina always talks about you, Kelsey. I know you two have become close lately. I don't want her to think I killed her mom."

"That's what Jason said, too. Why does everyone think Tina and I are so close?"

"She talks about you all the time. She looks up to you. I know when I hired you, it was just for personal training, but to her, you've become so much more. She talks about you like you're her mentor or an older sister."

"Okay, I'll take the bait," Kelsey said. "I'm interested in what you have to say, especially if it helps us find Anna's killer."

Chapter 31

Nick took a minute to compose himself, then explained his side of the story. He and Anna were introduced to one another by Leo Eriksen. Leo was married to Nick's sister Mae. He fell in love with Anna immediately. Her wild, carefree nature was a refreshing balance to his wound-up demeanor. She was only nineteen years old when they first met. They were married the following year. Then, Anna became pregnant at twenty-three. They were happy together for the first five years of Tina's life, but over time, it became apparent that Anna had some psychological issues. She started becoming paranoid that someone was out to get her.

"I think she had PTSD from her childhood," Nick said. "She would hide money and little notes to herself. I would find bundled cash hidden in drawers, underneath the fridge, in the area that held her car jack. I was scared she was developing schizophrenia. Anna was a wonderful, responsible mom before this all started. I know there was a little part of her that was worried as well. She couldn't explain it."

"When did you find out that Tina is not your biological daughter?" Kelsey asked.

"Anna called me to tell me about DNA tests she and Tina had taken. She said she didn't want to keep any secrets from me. I admit I was livid. I yelled and screamed at her on the phone when she told me. I called her a liar. I couldn't believe Anna would do that to me. How could Tina not be mine?"

"Do you think she knew she was pregnant with another man's baby?" Justin asked.

"I have no idea. I thought Anna loved me," Nick said, closing his eyes and shaking his head. "I never questioned anything she did at the beginning of our relationship. I thought we were happy. And yes. I've hit her. Dealing with her paranoia was difficult. She was so irrational at times. I'm deeply ashamed of the way I acted."

"Did you have money problems when you and Anna were together?" Justin asked. "Did she feel like she couldn't trust you with money? Do you think that's why she hid the money?"

"We both worked, her parttime a couple of days a week and me fulltime. We only shared some of the finances. We had separate bank accounts and one joint account. To her, there was never enough money. She always wanted more. She started questioning what I spent money on, even though we had plenty to live on. I liked to gamble online. After a long day at work, it was my only escape from reality. She would have a fit when she saw me at the computer playing poker. Her obsession with money spiraled out of control. I believe it was mainly because of her upbringing. Leo said when they were younger, she often came to their house to eat because there wasn't anything at home. After Anna and I separated, I checked in with her every week. She would invite me in for a glass of wine, and we would talk about Tina. We were amicable. One of the reasons I enrolled Tina in personal training along with many other activities is that I wanted her around Anna as little as possible. She was eighteen when I signed her up with you, Kelsey. Do you remember?"

Kelsey nodded, remembering that day like it was yesterday.

"Tina knew there wasn't something right with Anna, but she loved her mom. I told Tina my home would always be her home, no matter what. She didn't need to get caught in the middle of the drama between me and Anna. She could live wherever she wanted to. She was just a kid," Nick said with a tear in his eye.

"Okay, so I guess the question is, if you didn't kill Anna, then who did?" Kelsey said. "Who else has a motive?"

"That's what I want to find out, too. Who would kill Anna? I promise you both, it wasn't me. I can't keep hiding. I need your help to prove I'm innocent. I can't think of anything that would put me at the crime scene at the time of her murder. Of course, my DNA would be in the house, but that doesn't prove anything."

"I'm unclear why you don't just talk to the police. If you didn't do it, you have nothing to hide. Why not clear your name?" Kelsey asked.

"There are things I've done that I'm not proud of but that I'm trying to fix," Nick said.

Kelsey and Justin looked at each other in horror. Was he going to confess that he *did* murder Anna?

"No, no, I didn't kill her. I didn't kill anyone. There are some private things that I'm trying to work through."

"Other than the fact that Tina isn't your biological daughter?" Kelsey asked.

"Yes, other than that. It's something I can get in deep trouble for. I'm stuck."

"Kelsey and I need to sit down and process everything you've told us tonight if that's okay. Is there a way we can reach you?" Justin asked.

"I only have a burner phone, but you can call me on it as long as you promise not to give it to anyone."

"Sure, that sounds good," said Justin. Kelsey grabbed a pen and a piece of paper and placed them on the table in front of Mr. Scott. She and Justin held their breaths and exhaled as Mr. Scott took the pen in his right hand.

"Where are you staying for the time being?" Justin asked while Kelsey took another piece of paper to write their numbers down.

"I'd love to tell you guys, but please understand; I don't trust anyone right now."

"I get it, Mr. Scott. It's okay. Can you at least tell us where you were the night Anna was murdered?" Kelsey asked.

"I'm sorry. I can't," he said, looking down.

Chapter 32

Fox Fitness was buzzing Saturday morning. The cleaning service came early, and the machines were sparkly clean. As Kelsey passed the cardio machines, she noticed Josh deadlifting. Finley pulled her over to Saffron, who squealed with delight, taking Fin's leash.

"Hi, Kelsey! How are you? I was hoping you'd be here this morning," Josh said. "I just got off shift a couple of hours ago and thought I'd get a workout in before heading home to get some shut-eye. I have tonight off, so I was wondering if you'd like to grab a bite later."

"I would love to. What are you thinking?" Kelsey asked, her stomach doing a little somersault. *Date two? Yes!*

"I like pretty much everything. You pick. I know you're a foodie, so wherever you decide, I'm game. I don't have any allergies."

Kelsey took a chance and asked Josh if he liked sushi. She was pleasantly surprised that he did and was open to trying just about anything. A fantastic place in town called Kyoto's carried the freshest fish there was. After making plans for Josh to pick Kelsey up at six, Josh returned to deadlifting, and Kelsey prepared for her first client of the day. With a few minutes to spare, she sent a quick text.

hey, how are u today? miss u

Chapter 33

Saturday, September 24, 2022

Tina sat in a warm and cozy cabin in a small coastal town a few miles north of Santa Cruz. The smell of the sea air drifted through the cracked window as she lay on the bed reading an old beat up copy of *Wuthering Heights*. Yawning, Tina looked at the time on her phone. 7:55 a.m. As she did this, her phone pinged with a text.

hey, how are u today? miss u

I miss u 2! What are u doing?

about to start training. thinking of u tho.

same. They gave me some dumbbells, so maybe I'll do a workout.

maybe?

HAHA. Okay, I will.

Remember what I said about using a dumbbell as a weapon? Anyone tries to come at u and u whack'em with it.

yep. best weapon ever.

LOL. Okay, popping into a session. Talk later?

[thumbs up emoji] xoxo

Just then, there was a knock at the door.

"Tina, it's Tommy. We're doing a breakfast run. The guys voted on Mama's Café today. Would you like something?" a voice said through the door.

Tina opened the door to find Tommy, the security guard, standing on the front porch smiling at her. Tommy, Gino, Jeff, and Ethan were the four security guards assigned to patrol the grounds around the cabin, but Tommy was Tina's favorite because he always asked her if she wanted food. He also snuck her a bottle of wine the other night, knowing how bored she was.

"Hi, Tommy! Sure. Could I get the chicken and waffles, please?"

"You got it. Anything to drink?

"Yes, a vanilla latte, please. Can I Venmo you?"

Tommy waved his hand at her and said, "Don't worry about it. I've got you," the deep dimple in his cheek appearing as he smiled at her.

Smiling back, Tina replied, "Thanks, Tommy. That's so sweet of you."

Tina decided to do a quick workout. She sure missed Kelsey. She did a few dumbbell rows, followed by a set of bicep curls. Her muscles were tight, and she knew she needed this. As she lifted the dumbbells and felt the blood rush through her body, her heart rate rising, Tina's thoughts about her mom consumed her. *Did her mom do something in the past to make someone mad? Or was someone jealous of her?*

Chapter 34

Saturday, September 24, 2022

"So, what do you like here? I like sushi, but I've always gone with people who have ordered it for me," Josh said.

"Everything I've eaten here has been excellent. I like starting with the gyoza potstickers and then sharing a few rolls. Their Lion King and New York rolls are delicious. The Lion King is like a California roll with salmon and garlic sauce on top. It's baked so it melts in your mouth. The New York roll is a shrimp tempura roll with avocado and cucumber. They put crunchy tempura pieces on top. I also like the hamachi roll. It's simple and has hamachi and avocado in it," Kelsey explained.

"All of those sound like I would like them. Let's do it," Josh said.

The server arrived at their table to take their order and returned with a large sake and two little sake cups.

"On the house. The owner says hello, Kelsey," the server said.

"Aww, that's so sweet. Please thank Mr. Takahashi for me and tell him I say hello," Kelsey said.

The server gave her a little bow in affirmation.

"You must come here often if the owner knows you by name," Josh said, looking impressed.

"My family comes here a lot. My dad loves this place. Maybe even more than I do."

"Hey, so I have a question for you. How long have you known Tina?" Josh asked Kelsey.

"I've been training her for about five years. We've become close over the past year, though. I invited her over for a girl's night at Saffron's, and she had a great time," Kelsey said, remembering how hanging out with Tina felt so natural that night. "I miss training her, but I want to make sure she's safe, so I get it, you know?" Kelsey took a deep breath and held back the tears that were about to emerge. Josh reached across the table and took her hand in his.

"It's okay. You can cry in front of me. I know this has been hard on you. It's hard not being able to see someone you were used to seeing, what? Two, three, four times a week?" Josh said, his voice full of empathy.

"Yeah, we train three times a week, but we also text back and forth constantly." *Shoot, that reminds me. I forgot to text her after pickleball.*

"Did you ever meet her mom, Anna?" Josh asked, and Kelsey wondered why Josh was suddenly so interested in Tina and her family.

"No, I'd never met her. Mr. Scott was the one who signed Tina up for training with me. I have a tough time believing he would hurt Tina. I mean, maybe he killed Anna because he was so mad that she had an affair and had a daughter with someone else, but I don't think that would make him mad at Tina. Tina didn't know he wasn't her real dad. Anna didn't even know that Tina wasn't his until recently."

"From what I've heard, all the evidence leads to Nick Scott being the murderer, Kelsey. There's no way he's getting away with it. He had to be the one who killed Anna. No one else has a motive."

Why was Josh being so adamant about Nick being the murderer? And he wasn't even working the case. How did he know what evidence they had?

Just then, the gyoza and sushi arrived at the table. Kelsey picked up a potsticker, her mouth, watering.

Josh started laughing, covering his mouth to try and stifle himself. Kelsey looked at him, confused. "What's so funny?" she said, looking around to see what he was laughing at.

"What were you thinking about just now, Kelsey? You had the biggest, goofiest smile on your face!" he said, laughing some more.

Kelsey could feel her face turn red in embarrassment and laughed, too. "Oh, you know, that was just my foodie face. I'm surprised you didn't notice it last time when we were at the pub. I have a serious love for good food. Justin and the girls at the gym always make fun of me for it." She cleared her throat and took a sip of water. "So, now you know something about me that most people don't. Well, until they eat with me, that is. So, tell me, what are your little quirks and pet peeves?"

Josh took another piece of the Lion King roll, thinking of what to say. After he swallowed, he said, "Well, I don't think I have anything as cute as your foodie face, but I guess my quirk would be that I'm very much a night owl. I have been since I was a little kid. I could stay up all night. My parents would come into my room and find me with a flashlight under the covers, reading a book or playing with action figures."

"Oh, come on, that's not weird at all! Okay, you'll have to work on coming up with a better quirk. That's your homework!"

He laughed, "Oh wow, it's only our second date, and you're already giving me homework!"

"It's due on our third date," Kelsey laughed. Despite the little outburst about Nick, she was having fun with Josh. He was good-looking and had a great sense of humor. And they never seemed to run out of things to talk about.

"I'm stuffed," Josh said.

"Me too. It was so good, though, right?"

"It was excellent," Josh said, reaching across the table for Kelsey's hands, and squeezing them gently. "Thank you for bringing me to your favorite sushi place. I hope we have many more dates here."

Kelsey grinned and said, "Me too."

They sat digesting their food and taking a few more sips of water. Kelsey looked at her phone. 7:45.

"Hey, do you want to go to The Pirate Ship? It's a super cool bar down the street. We can grab a drink and talk some more."

"Sure," Josh replied. "The Pirate Ship, huh? That sounds like it could be fun."

Excusing herself to the ladies' room, Kelsey sent Tina a quick text.

Hey, I didn't forget about you. I'm on a date with one of my dad's coworkers. I can't wait to tell you all about him.

Omg, that's so exciting! Can't wait to hear about your date. Go have fun! xoxo

XOXO

Kelsey and Josh strolled down to The Pirate Ship, a cool, trendy bar decked out in pirate flags, treasure, and statues of pirates. They had your standard run-of-the-mill drinks and a special menu with pirate-themed drinks like "Argh, who goes there" and "Shiver me Timbers."

"Oh wow, this is awesome," Josh said, taking in all the decor.

"I know. Like *Pirates of the Caribbean*. That's my favorite ride at Disneyland."

"I've never been to Disneyland, but I heard it's magical. And, of course, I've seen all the *Pirates* movies."

"What?" Kelsey said, in disbelief. "What do you mean you've never been to Disneyland?"

"I know. I'm probably the only person who hasn't ever been. My sister and I would spend our summers at the lake instead of going on traditional family vacations. My parents worked a lot because they owned an Italian restaurant on the pier. It's a hot spot in Seattle. They worked hard to build the business from the ground up. I took care of my sister a lot so they could do that." Looking down at the menu, he said, "So, what in the world is a 'Davy Jones Locker'?"

"That one will have you three sheets to the wind. It's like a Long Island Iced Tea but even stronger, if that's possible. Trust me, stick to the regular drinks you know. Melissa is the bartender tonight. She makes the drinks extra strong."

"All right, I trust you. I don't need to be three sheets to the wind. Ever."

"Yeah, I—" but before Kelsey could complete her sentence, he leaned over and gently kissed her. Kelsey could feel her whole body stiffen, her stomach tingly with butterflies. "That was nice," she said.

"Well, hey there, Kels! What's kickin'? Are you going to introduce me to your friend here?" Melissa said as she came toward them. She poured them each a glass of ice water.

"Hey, Mel!" Kelsey greeted her and stood up on the rung of her barstool to reach over the bar for a hug. Melissa was a single mom who Kelsey met at Fox nine years ago. A hard worker, Melissa did her best to work and spend time with her son, Miles. Her boyfriend, Miles's dad, Levi, passed away in a terrible car accident on the freeway. A garbage truck had been going the wrong way and hit him, killing him instantly.

"This is my friend Josh. He works with my dad. He's from Seattle."

"Very cool. I took Miles to Seattle for a little trip a couple of years ago. We went to see the Space Needle and to Chihuly Gardens. He loved it," Melissa said to Josh.

"Miles is her son," Kelsey told Josh. Then she turned to Melissa, "How old is Miles now? Twelve?"

"Yep. Next year, he'll be a teenager. I can't believe how fast time goes." She smiled. "What can I get you two? Did Kelsey tell you about the drinks on the menu? I think she's tried them all." Melissa smirked.

"Hey now, don't make me sound like a lush. I have a reputation to uphold."

"Oh, like your reputation of having a funny foodie face?" Mel said, now starting to really laugh.

"You know about that face too? I just saw it for the first time tonight!" Josh joined in and he and Melissa started laughing like it was the funniest thing in the world.

"Okay, okay, haha, very funny. Joke's on Kelsey. Always the butt of the joke. I get it," Kelsey said, making a pretend mad face.

After they finished their laughing fit, Kelsey said, "I think I'll just have a glass of Sauvignon Blanc."

Josh said, "That sounds good. I'll have the same."

"You got it. Do you guys want snacks?" Mel asked as she took down two glasses and poured their wine. "We have those cool little twisty pretzels you like, Kels."

"Seasoned or plain?"

"They sent us both this time," Mel said. "We have almonds too. The wasabi ones."

"Yes, please. We'll take some of the seasoned pretzels and wasabi almonds. Do you have the wasabi peas, too?

"We sure do!" Melissa said as she scurried off to get the snacks from the back.

"Sounds like this is your home away from home. Every drink on the menu, huh?" Josh asked Kelsey, raising one eyebrow.

"She's exaggerating. I've probably tried almost every drink but it's only because I've come here with friends, and we all try each other's drinks. I don't like gin, so I don't know what those drinks taste like."

"Ahh, got it," Josh said. "I'm not a huge gin fan either. I got sick from it when I was a teenager, and now I can't even smell it without feeling queasy."

Melissa came back with the snacks, and all three stopped what they were doing to watch the special news alert that popped up on the big screen TV.

"And now, breaking news from our Fox News Center. Nicholas Scott, who is wanted for questioning in connection with the homicide of his ex-wife Anna Scott, has turned himself into the Oakview Police Department. We have Chief of Police Randy James here with a statement."

Randy James came on and spoke, "Mr. Scott is currently in our custody. We will be questioning him thoroughly and will keep everyone posted with updates on the case. Thank you."

Chapter 35

B *ang! Bang! Bang!*

Kelsey's head pounded harder as the banging on her door got louder. Getting out of bed, shuffling into her slippers, and grabbing her phone, she found Finley waiting at the door. She threw the door open and shouted, "What?"

"Kels! Why weren't you answering your phone?" Justin said as he pushed past her into the condo.

"Justin! It's six in the freaking morning! On a Sunday!" Kelsey said, rubbing the sleep out of her eyes. She grabbed a bottle of water from the fridge and chugged it down.

"Did you see the news this morning? Tina's dad is in custody."

"Yeah, I know. I saw that on the news last night while at the Pirate Ship. I don't know why he did that." She sat down on one of the barstools and put her head in her hands. "Can you get me the Advil on the counter over there, Jus? My head is throbbing."

"Did you talk to your dad?" Justin asked. Handing her the Advil, he started making a pot of coffee. "And what did you drink last night? You smell like a keg of something! It's practically oozing out of your pores!" He leaned over to sniff her, and she pushed him away and giggled.

"I am so hungover. Do I smell that bad?" Kelsey asked, sniffing her armpits. "I haven't talked to my dad, but I should probably get that coffee into my body and then shower. You want to come with me to my parents' house after the farmers' market?"

Justin poured two big mugs of coffee and put almond milk in both.

"Yeah, I'll come. We need to pick your dad's brain for info on Mr. Scott. Did you tell your dad we talked to him?"

"No. I don't know why Mr. Scott would turn himself in. I'll be so mad if he lied to us, and he was the one who murdered Anna."

Just then, a new text pinged on Kelsey's phone.

I TOLD YOU TO MIND YOUR OWN BUSINESS. NOW LOOK WHAT YOU'VE DONE.

Chapter 36

Sunday, September 25, 2022

Justin and Kelsey stared at the text. Who was sending them? And what was it exactly that Kelsey had done? As she compared the new text to the old one, Kelsey saw it came from the same number, one based out of Oakview, California. Wondering if the police could do something to find out who owned the phone or if it was an untraceable burner, Kelsey decided to show her dad the ominous threats.

Relaxing under the hot shower, Kelsey opened a new bottle of shampoo—berries and vanilla. The scent made her think about summertime desserts and how she couldn't wait for the weather to warm up again. Getting out of the shower, she threw on some comfy Sunday sweats and walked out into the kitchen, her hair still damp but combed through. She finished her second cup of coffee, which had gone cold by now, and walked over to the couch to put on her socks and shoes. "Ready, guys?" she asked Justin and Finley. They ambled out of the condo and hopped into Chuckie.

Justin picked through the organic herbs from Stanley's Farm in Hollister, California. Their herbs had the best aroma and flavor of any of the local growers. Justin collected a bunch of Italian parsley, tarragon, and rosemary, and gently placed them in plastic bags. He thought to himself, *Kelsey would love some roasted potatoes with rosemary. I'll pair that with some lamb chops.* He caught up to Kelsey and Fin who were at the hummus booth. Kelsey was helping herself to each of the dip samples. "Here, try this one, Justin," she said, shoveling a piece of pita into his mouth. "It's spicy garlic. Isn't that good?"

Before Justin could respond, Kelsey saw her client, Caroline, walking their way.

"Hi, Caro! How are you?" Kelsey said, hugging her.

"Kelsey! What a beautiful day for the market. This is my daughter Audrey."

"Hi, it's so nice to meet you," Kelsey said, shaking Audrey's hand. Audrey was about 5'8" with long, wavy brown hair, fringy bangs, and brown eyes. And gorgeous.

"Nice to meet you, too. I have been meaning to message you. My mom raves about her sessions with you. And I have to say, Mom's looking pretty good!" Audrey said with a big smile.

"I didn't know you two were dating! How wonderful!" Caroline said to Kelsey and Justin.

"Oh, no, we're not," Kelsey said, blushing. "We're just good friends. We hang out a lot. You know how it is at the gym, Caroline. We're like one big family. Audrey, this is Justin. He trains at Fox also."

"It's nice to meet you, Justin," Audrey said, and Kelsey could see a twinkle in her eye as she made eye contact with him.

"Nice to meet you, too," Justin said, smiling at Audrey. Then, Justin turned his attention to Kelsey and said, "We'd better get going if we're going to bring this stuff back to your place and then go to your parents."

"Right. We'd better go. Oh, and Audrey, feel free to message me anytime. We can do a free consultation and fitness assessment if you'd like. There's no pressure, though." Kelsey handed Audrey her card as Justin walked away with Finley in search of more fine produce.

"Fantastic. Now, I have no excuse not to go to the gym. I see you have a scheduling app link on here. Should I go to that and book an appointment?" Audrey asked.

"Yes, pick a spot that works for you," Kelsey said. "I'll see you next week, Caro. And nice meeting you, Audrey!"

"Hey, wait up!" Kelsey said as she noticed Justin was already five booths ahead of her.

"Audrey seemed nice," Kelsey said, looking at Justin to see his reaction. "She sure is pretty."

"She looked familiar. Hey, I want to start making more soups. What do you think of potato leek? Maybe with a little chive garnish on top." Justin paused, then said, "I don't know why I'm asking you this. I could roll a potato in the dirt, and you'd eat it."

"Probably! So, do you think you know her?"

"Who?"

"Justin! Do you think you know Caro's daughter?"

"I don't know. Her face just looked familiar. Like I've seen her before."

"You should ask her out."

"Hmm. Yeah, she's okay. I don't know if I'm ready to start dating again yet, but I'm satisfied with my life right now. I have everything I need," Justin said, smiling at Kelsey and handing her Finley's leash.

Justin finished up his shopping while Kelsey took samples of English cucumbers from under a plastic dome.

She ate one, gave one to Finley, and then stuffed one into Justin's mouth.

"Mmmmph. Kelsey, what is this?" Justin asked, his mouth open as if he were afraid to eat it.

"It's a cucumber! Don't you trust me by now, Justin? It's not like I would put a raw potato in your mouth," Kelsey replied with a smirk.

Justin ate the cucumber and mumbled, "Brat."

Chapter 37

Sunday, September 25, 2022

J oanna sat at the kitchen table in her bathrobe, a steamy cup of coffee in front of her. She was pleased with the latest reviews of her new mystery, released only two weeks ago. Her agent did an exemplary job of finding new outlets to market her book. As she took a sip from her mug, she heard the front door squeak open, followed by a little clitter clatter headed in her direction. She looked down to see Finley at her feet.

"Well, hello there, my sweet grandpup!" she said, bending to pet Finley. "What a pleasant surprise! Kelsey, Justin, to whom do I owe this pleasure? I was about to make some breakfast for Brian. Would you like some?"

"Hi, Mom. Sorry to drop in like this. I need to talk to Dad. Is he not home?" Kelsey asked as Joanna stood up to start cooking.

"Oh, no, I'm sorry you just missed him. He was up and out of here about fifteen minutes ago. He had to go to the station. You heard Tina's dad turned himself in?"

"Sit back down and finish your coffee, Mom. I'll get breakfast going." Kelsey opened the fridge and pulled out the eggs, bacon, and Irish butter. She handed the bacon to Justin, who had already started warming the cast iron pan.

"That's why we're here. I was hoping we could catch him and find out what was happening. I didn't tell Dad, but Justin and I talked to Mr. Scott a few days ago. Justin and I don't think he did it, Mom. We think he's being set up."

"Oh, Kelsey, I wish you wouldn't get stuck in the middle of all this. I don't want to see anything happen to either of you. It's best to leave things like this up to your dad and the department," Joanna worried.

"That's what I've been trying to tell her, Mrs. James. There could be a killer out there, but who knows what his next move will be. That's the whole reason Tina is in custody—to protect her in case her life is in danger," Justin said.

Kelsey snarled and threw him a dirty look. "Thanks for the support, partner. You're not helping."

Brian came flopping down the stairs in his Mario Brothers pajamas, which were too short for him. "Yum, something smells good. Bacon! Gimme bacon!" he said in his hungry bacon monster voice, his eyes still half closed from sleep.

"Morning, Bri!" Kelsey said.

"Hi, Kels! Hi, Justin! What are you guys doing here?" he said, rubbing his eyes. Then, he saw Fin. "Fin! Hi, buddy! How's my favorite doggy?" Brian sat on the floor next to Finley and leaned over to hug him. Finley gave Brian a little lick on the chin. Sometimes, he went up to Brian's room, and they lounged on the mini couch Brian sat on while playing his video games. They were like two peas in a pod. Finley loved cuddling up next to Brian.

"We wanted to talk to Dad about something related to his work, but he's not here, so Justin and I are helping Mom make breakfast."

"Mmm," Brian mumbled as he plopped himself down on the chair next to Justin and leaned on the kitchen table. "What's up, Justin? Have you played any new games lately? I haven't seen you in the Discord recently."

"Nah, I've been working so much and helping Kelsey with this thing we're working on that I haven't had time. I heard the new COD is pretty killer, though. Did you get it?" Justin replied.

"Yeah, I got it. It's pretty legit. You can come up to my room to play it if you want. I got it on PS5. Is that thing you're working on with Kelsey, the murder thing about Tina's mom? Are you guys trying to solve the case?" Brian asked, his eyes getting bigger in excitement. Kelsey looked over at Brian, surprised. For a kid who usually didn't say much, he sure did pick up on a lot.

"Well," Justin said, "I'm just trying to keep your sister out of trouble. So even though she thinks I'm helping her, I'm really just trying to protect her."

"Uh, hello!" Kelsey said. "Standing right here. And shut up, Justin. You know you liked sneaking around in Tina's house and going through Jason's phone just as much as I did."

Justin laughed, "Okay, that was pretty fun. But we do need to watch our step. Neither of us think Tina's dad did it, and in that case, the killer is still on the loose."

"Hey, you know Tina is our sister, right, Kels?" Brian blurted out suddenly.

"Yeah, I do. You know about that?"

"Yeah, remember? No secrets. That's our family pact."

Kelsey walked over to Brian and gave him a big hug.

"I love you, Bri," she said with wet eyes. "You're the best brother anyone could have." Brian gave her back a big bear hug and then rolled his eyes. "Don't worry, Kels. You'll always be my favorite sister. I won't like Tina more than you."

Kelsey tickled him, making him go into a laughing fit. "I'd better be your favorite sister forever! Or else!"

Kelsey felt her phone buzz in her pocket just then. It was a text from her dad.

I have some interesting news regarding Nick Scott. Do you have a minute?

Chapter 38

Sunday, September 25, 2022

As Justin and Kelsey buzzed into the police station's front desk, they heard Randy yelling in his office. Fin whimpered, and Kelsey bent down, scratched him behind his ears, and said, "It's okay, boy. Grandpa's just doing some serious business."

As they approached Randy's office, he was saying something about "four guards being necessary." It sounded like someone had crossed him. Kelsey was glad she wasn't on the other side of that conversation.

Kelsey peeked into the office door. "Dad?"

"Hey, sweetie. Sorry about that. Here, you guys come in. Shut the door. I want to talk to you. I'm glad you're both here," he said. "Nick Scott has an alibi the night Anna was killed."

"Wait, what? Why? How? Why didn't he say that from the beginning?" Kelsey asked.

"Everything that you hear in this room today stays here. No one—and I mean no one—is allowed this information. I haven't told any of the other officers about it. Only Hart knows. We have no other suspects."

"But what's his alibi?" Justin asked.

"He was with his boss, Dalton Brooks. They were at a bar in San Francisco at the time of Anna's murder. We have camera footage from the bar. It's him on the camera that night."

"A bar? With his boss? What's so bad about that?" Kelsey said, bewildered.

"It wasn't so much the fact that they were at a bar as it is why they were there," Randy continued. "Nick and Dalton were there to participate in an illegal poker game. The clientele was elite, and the stakes were high. An investment group rented the back room. It's by invitation only. And get this: Nick Scott owes big money in gambling debts. We aren't sure how much, but it's enough for someone to have a bounty on him."

"Kind of like in *Molly's Game*?" Kelsey said, thinking about her all-time favorite Jessica Chastain movie in which she played Molly Bloom, a woman notorious for building and operating the world's largest underground high-stakes poker game. "So, that's where he was? Will he get in trouble for the illegal gambling?"

"We cut him a deal. He's working for us now and has agreed to tell the FBI everything he knows about the group in exchange for immunity. We need Nick to be our eyes and ears for anything happening with the family. We're not announcing any of this to the public, of course. For all we care, he can tell people he was out at a bar and leave it at that," Randy said. "Furthermore, we discovered that Anna was helping Nick pay off his gambling debt."

"Why would he kill her if she was helping him?" Kelsey stated. "Tina said her mom's company was doing well and that her parents had been getting along fine. Nick doesn't have a strong enough motive for killing her. I knew he was telling the truth the other night!"

"Kels, what do you mean the other night? Did you talk to Nick Scott?" Randy said, his face getting red.

Kelsey froze in her seat. Justin turned to look at her.

"Uhh. Yeah, that's why we went over to the house. We were going to tell you about Mr. Scott's visit a few nights ago," Kelsey said, her voice hoarse.

"Kelsey Sue James!" Randy's voice boomed and ricocheted off the office walls. "I do not need you and Justin to be the next murder victims! I am sharing this information with you because you are my daughter, and Tina is my daughter, and it is my job to keep you both safe. But, so help me God, if you do anything as dangerous as talking to a possible murderer ever again, I will lock you up and throw away the key!"

"I'm sorry, Dad. I just wanted to help."

Randy walked over to Kelsey and picked her up from her chair by her shoulders. Throwing her into a big bear hug, he put his chin on her head.

Finally, Justin said, "I'm sorry, Mr. James. We wanted to tell you, but we also wanted to gain Mr. Scott's trust."

"I understand, Justin. But you need to keep me in the loop with things like this."

"Understood, sir."

"I have something that might interest you, Dad," Kelsey said, trying to change the subject.

"What's that?" Randy asked, raising an eyebrow.

"I was going through a box of Anna's family photos, and there was a baby picture. It was dated September, 1990. Did Anna ever mention having a baby other than Tina?"

"No, she never mentioned that."

"Tina wasn't born until 1999, so the picture couldn't have been of her."

"Interesting. She didn't talk much about her life growing up. I knew very little about her parents or if she even had any siblings. She never wanted to talk about any of that. We mostly talked about what we wanted for the future. I think it was then that I realized that I didn't want to cheat on your mom anymore and that I had made a big mistake by getting involved with someone like Anna. Anna and I wanted different things out of life. She was a very fly-by-the-seat-of-her-pants kind of woman. She loved being spontaneous, and hopped from job to job. Nick must have paid for just about everything back then. Anna and I had fun, but I knew nothing could top the life I led with your mom, and I recognized my stupidity. I love your mom and was in lust with this woman. Thinking about that time in my life, I was so confused. And for no good reason. I had it all. A wonderful life, a beautiful daughter, a budding career. Why would I want to mess that up? I'm glad I got my head out of my ass because if I hadn't, then maybe Brian wouldn't have been born."

"Okay, so we know someone killed Anna on Tuesday night. Mr. Scott was at an illegal poker game. Tina was hanging out with her cousin, Jason, at an arcade and came home and found her mom. Abby and David were out to dinner. We have proof of that. That leaves Leo and Aunt Mae. Do either of them have a motive to kill Anna? And do they all have alibis?"

"That's the recap for now, kiddo. We're still in the process of bringing the family in for interviews. He's having a difficult time getting a hold of Leo and Mae. He's also been interviewing everyone on the block to see if they saw anything suspicious that evening. So far, no witnesses have turned up, but there are several houses whose owners he has been unable to contact."

Kelsey pulled her phone out to show Randy the ominous text messages she had received. There was a new notification—a text from the same number.

YOUR DADDY WON'T ALWAYS BE THERE TO PROTECT YOU.

Chapter 39

Monday, September 26, 2022

During her midday break, Kelsey climbed into Chuckie and immediately cranked up the heater to full blast, seeking warmth. The fall air was so cold it had left her with a permanent chill down her spine. Kelsey pulled her phone out and dialed a number, her breath visible in the cold air.

"Hello?"

"Hey, Jason?"

"Yeah, hi, Kelsey. How's it going? Did you find out any more info about my Aunt Anna's murder? I heard my Uncle Nick turned himself in."

"Yeah, he's still with the police. I have an update on Tina. She's safe. After she left your grandparents' house, she went straight to the police department."

"What? Where is she? Is she okay? What did she say?"

"She's fine. The police have her in protective custody."

"Oh, thank God," Jason said.

"Do you know why your Aunt Mae and Uncle Leo won't cooperate with the police? It's a little shady if you ask me,"

Kelsey asked, hoping Jason would give her insight into what was happening with the pair.

"I'm not sure. I wouldn't put it past either of them to know more than they're letting on. It might be that they don't trust anyone and are keeping secrets. I haven't spoken to either of them in a few days."

"Do you think Leo would talk to me? Maybe we could all meet somewhere?"

"I don't know. My uncle was acting weird last week. He's been anxious and fidgety. In the last conversation we had, he said he's going to find Anna's killer because the police aren't doing their job."

"Why does he care about this so much? Why not just let the police do their job?"

"My Uncle Leo knew Anna before she married my Uncle Nick. His sister was Anna's best friend. I think, in a lot of ways, this is his way of mourning Anna. He loved her like a little sister. He comes off as gruff and mean, but he has a good heart, even though he can be a little psycho at times. I think Anna's death has torn him apart."

"That makes a lot of sense. Could you try asking your uncle if he'll meet us?"

"But didn't my Uncle Nick already turn himself in? He's guilty, right?"

"I don't know what he's told the police," Kelsey lied, "but I talked to him a few nights ago, and he swore that he didn't do it. I don't know what would have changed between then and now."

"You talked to my Uncle Nick?" Jason said, surprised.

"He broke into my condo, which scared the crap out of me, but then I agreed to sit down and listen to his side of the story. He didn't seem violent or angry, just desperate to clear his name."

"I see. Okay, let me talk to Leo and see what he says. If Nick isn't the killer, then we have a big problem. I don't know who else would want to hurt my Aunt Anna, let alone kill her."

"I agree. Where did your Aunt Anna work? Maybe we should start asking her coworkers if they knew anything. Or what about her friends?"

"Tina never really talked about her mom's job or friends. I'm not sure. You'd have to ask her or my Uncle Nick," Jason said.

"I wish I had thought of it that night when we spoke to your Uncle Nick. Well, the sooner I talk to Leo, the better. We all need to put our brains together to figure this out."

Chapter 40

Monday, September 26, 2022

Thoughts of everything that could go wrong about meeting with Kelsey James took over Leo's brain. Why did Jason think getting the police chief's daughter involved in their family affairs was a good idea? Over the years, Leo had several encounters with the police and didn't trust them as far as the eye could see.

"You know she's the police chief's daughter, don't you?" Leo said, questioning his nephew. Jason was a good kid, but he wasn't necessarily the sharpest. He was easily influenced and naïve to the ways of the world.

"I know. But she's not working for the police. She wants to help find out who killed Anna," Jason told his uncle. "It's why Tina likes her so much. I think she's a good person. Plus, maybe she knows something we don't."

"What about Tina? Did you find out where she is? Is she okay?"

"The police are protecting her."

"Okay, that's good. That's good," Leo said. "Fine. We'll meet Kelsey. But you let me do the talking. Have your mom book a hotel room at the Summerfield Suites. We'll meet there."

Chapter 41

Monday, September 26, 2022

Kelsey entered the police station and headed to the conference room. She was surprised to receive a call from Jason letting her know his uncle was willing to speak to her, however, she was a little skeptical they booked a hotel room instead of agreeing on a public meeting place. She knew she had to have faith her dad's crew would be ready to pounce if anything untoward happened.

Randy introduced Kelsey to the department's tech specialist, Robert Davis, who fitted her with a quarter-sized microphone. They placed the sensitive device in the small zipper pocket on the side of her backpack. The device would allow them to hear everything Kelsey and Leo said, but because an earpiece would be bulky and give the surveillance away, she wouldn't be able to hear the officers.

Kelsey took her notebook out of her bag and flipped it open. "Okay, I'm ready for questions."

Chapter 42

Monday, September 26, 2022

The hotel sliding glass doors opened to the main lobby, and Kelsey was hit with the light scent of citrus. Waiting for the elevator, she took several deep breaths and tried to calm her nerves. She double-checked the little metal disk in her backpack as the elevator zipped up to the third floor. Her phone dinged.

Stop touching the mic. It's extremely sensitive. Don't worry—you'll do great, Dad.

Ok. Sorry.

She knocked on room 313, and Jason answered the door. Kelsey gave a sigh of relief when she realized she didn't have to meet with Leo alone.

"Hi, Kelsey. C'mon in," Jason said, smiling.

She entered the hotel room, and a stocky man over six feet tall stood near a small table in the corner, holding a glass of whiskey. Wearing a gray pinstriped suit with a white dress shirt and black wing-tipped dress shoes, he reminded Kelsey of a movie gangster.

"Kelsey, meet Leo. Uncle Leo, this is Kelsey."

"Hello, Kelsey. It's good to meet you. I'm sorry it's under these circumstances. I hear you want to help us find Anna's killer. That's great news. All I want is to protect my family and to bring Anna's killer to justice. My niece, Tina, speaks very highly of you. I don't want any trouble." He gestured for her to sit down at the table.

"It's nice to meet you too, Leo. Thanks for agreeing to talk to me," Kelsey said, shaking his hand and then taking a seat.

"Would you like something to drink? We have a bottle of MacAllen, Grey Goose, and water and sodas," Leo said.

"I'm okay. I brought water with me," Kelsey said as she leaned over to take her notebook and pen out.

"Very well. Before we start, I have a question for you. Are you working for the police?" he asked, his expression like stone.

"Why would you ask me that?" Kelsey said, feeling the pit of her stomach form into a rock. *Is he not going to cooperate after all?*

Leo clasped his hands in front of him and leaned forward. "Kelsey, let me be straight with you. And I hope that you are with me as well. Like I said, I don't want any trouble. I know the police are looking for me to interview, so maybe I'll contact them when I'm ready. Mae and I have always treated Jason and Tina as if they were our very own children. All I want is to find Anna's killer."

"Well, that's why I'm here. To help Tina find her mother's killer. I know you were close to Anna. I want to help."

"You're also the police chief's daughter, so that's why I'm asking. Are you working for the police? Do I have to worry about them storming in here and arresting me?"

"They know I'm here with you. I don't know that they would have a reason to arrest you. I have only a few questions," Kelsey explained.

Leo nodded. "I understand. I'm hoping I can trust you, Kelsey. We have the same goal, after all. I don't know if Jason told you, but Anna was like a little sister to me. I introduced her and Nick. I need to say this before we start, but I do have a license to conceal and carry, so I do. I just thought you might want to know that. If we keep things honest and friendly, then there is no problem. It is for personal protection only. Are we clear?" He opened his jacket a little to reveal a holstered Smith & Wesson.

Chapter 43

Transcript of Leo Eriksen's conversation with Kelsey James

Kelsey: Who knew about Tina being at the Scotts' house?

Leo: Well, Jason here, of course. His parents, Abby and David. And Mae. Sadie and Bill [Scott] knew Tina was staying at the house. David told them she was having a hard time with her mom's death. We took turns bringing her food and stuff she needed from the house.

Kelsey: So, Mae, you, and Jason. Are you all close to Tina *and* Anna?

Leo: Yeah, I mean, I guess. We like having family barbecues and that sort of thing. The Scotts are nice people. They're very generous. They love their kids and their grandkids. At first, Mae and Anna didn't really hit it off. Mae is the real jealous kind. But I've known Anna for most of my life and I introduced her and Nick. Mae and Anna have become closer over the years.

Kelsey: Was there anyone you can think of who would want to hurt Anna?

Leo: No. Anna was a sweet lady. She had a hard upbringing, so she was always over at my house because she was my sister Carla's best friend. She spent the night all the time. Those two were inseparable. I think she was probably over at our house more than her own.

Kelsey: Does she still keep in touch with Carla?

Leo: Nah, I don't think so. My sister moved to Las Vegas to attend college and ended up staying.

She became a realtor. I only see her during the holidays. Usually, Mae and I fly out there for Christmas and New Year's. She's married to a great guy, and they have two kids in their teens.

She's doing well.

Kelsey: That's great. How old were Anna and Carla when they were friends?

Leo: Probably middle school and high school? I believe they lost touch after high school. Why the interest in my sister?

Kelsey: I'm just trying to learn a little more about Anna and her past. We don't know much about her at all.

Leo: Oh. I see. Okay, so how are we going to find out who killed her? I'll tell you now, it's not my sister.

Kelsey: No, no, I didn't think it was. I'm just trying to get a feel for Anna's life. Knowing her history, friends, relationships, etcetera, could help us. Okay, so back to Tina. You kept her at her grandparents' house. What did she tell you when she finally came to?

Leo: Well, she said that she wanted to go home. And she wanted to see her dad. Jason and I knew that was a bad idea because of her dad's temper, so we told her we thought it would be safer for her to stay with Mima and Pop Pop (that's the Scotts). She said she would wait a few days until this blew over, but that was it. As you know, Jason went to her house to grab some clothes and personal items for her, but he dropped his phone when he was there. Mae went back to find it but didn't.

Kelsey: Okay, great. Did Tina tell you anything else?

Leo: Nah. Not really.

Kelsey: What else can you tell us about Anna's past? You said she had a hard upbringing?

Leo: Yeah, her mom was unreliable and very flighty. She was never around. And her dad was heavy into the drink, although he worked and supported the family. He abandoned Anna and her mom, uh, that was probably right before high school. Anna always said she was scared of her dad. I know he physically abused her mother. Sometimes, Anna would come over to our place because there was no food at home. My parents loved having her over. My dad liked her better than either me or Carla. She was shy. Anna and Carla were good girls. They minded their manners and never caused any trouble. That changed when the girls got a little older, though. I guess you could say Anna was a little wild. Nothing too horrible. Just parties and drinking and stuff like that. Carla was the same. You know, regular teenage girl stuff. But something happened around their sophomore year. Anna stopped coming around after that.

Kelsey: What happened?

Leo: I don't know exactly, but rumor had it that she got pregnant and had to give the kid up. We didn't see her again until senior year. She and Carla talked still, but she didn't really come over

after that.

Kelsey: Do you think this could have something to do with her getting killed?

Leo: How should I know? It seems like forever ago.

Kelsey: Who was the father of her baby?

Leo: I don't know. Maybe some kid she went to school with? I was just the big brother. No one told me nothing. I just know she stopped coming around.

Kelsey: Did you ever ask her after she came back into your lives?

Leo: No. I figured she would have if she wanted to tell me or the family.

Kelsey: Okay, got it. So, do you know any of Anna's friends? Is there anyone she talked about?

Maybe a special someone she dated after Nick?

Leo: After she and Nick split, Anna kept to herself. She worked from home during the pandemic and only went into the office when she needed to after that. She was a real introvert, and I think she spent most of her time with Tina. Occasionally, she would come for family gatherings.

Kelsey: Did she talk about any coworkers or friends she would go out with before the split from Nick? Like even for drinks after work? That kind of thing.

Leo: Nah, Anna didn't drink. She used to. I know her paranoia was starting to get worse. Do you know about that?

Kelsey: I spoke to Nick briefly, and he mentioned it. Can you tell me a little more about that?

Leo: Sure, she would tell me she thought "they" were watching her. When I asked her who, she wouldn't tell me. She hid money, and Nick would tell Mae that he was worried she might be hallucinating that someone was after her.

Kelsey: I see. So, Anna had a good relationship with Nick after the divorce? And she got along with Abby and David? And she and Mae were friendly?

Leo: Yes, yes, and yes. You know what I think? It was a complete freak accident. I think she opened the door for a stranger, and that person intended to rob her. Anna would have fought back, though. I know her. She was small but mighty.

Kelsey: What about fingerprints, though? And if Anna fought back, there would have been blood or DNA from the perpetrator, right? Only Anna's blood was found at the scene. Plus, there was nothing stolen. The police recovered her purse, laptop, and phone.

Leo: You got me there, kid. What was the murder weapon, by the way? The police never said.

Kelsey: I'm not sure. The autopsy just said she was hit with a blunt object.

Leo: Well, whoever it was, I hope they're scared shitless right now.

Kelsey: One last question. Where were you and Mae the night of Anna's murder?

Leo: That's easy. I was at the Chase Bank on Third. I went home after that and did some banking on my computer. Mae stayed late at the courthouse library that night with a client. It wasn't us. We didn't kill Anna.

Kelsey: Okay, well, I think that's it for now. Thank you so much for meeting with me. I really appreciate it.

Leo: I just want to get to the bottom of this. Anna was very special to me. Like I said, she went through a lot when she was a kid.

Kelsey: Well, I'd like to keep in touch so we can keep you posted. My friend Justin and I are working on this together. Jason, you have my number.

Jason: Yeah, thanks a lot, Kelsey. Hopefully, the information Leo gave you will help.

Kelsey: Oh, wait. I have one more question. Did either of you text me to mind my own business?

Leo: Nope, I didn't.

Jason: No, it wasn't me. Who do you think it was?

Kelsey: I don't know, but someone's out there watching.

[End of interview].

Chapter 44

Tuesday, September 27, 2022

K elsey sat at her kitchen counter, nursing her second cup of coffee. She was ready for work early today on account of Justin calling her at 5:30 in the morning from Texas. He had flown out to visit his parents on Monday morning and had forgotten about the time difference. Realizing she had at least half an hour to kill, she pulled her notebook out and reviewed her interview notes again. Did Leo say anything that would point the finger at him killing Anna? The police would check out his and Mae's alibis, but he sounded confident when giving them. Excited to do more detective work, she called her dad who answered the phone on the first ring.

"Hi, Dad!"

"Hey, sweetie! I was going over the interview you had with Leo."

"Great. That's why I'm calling. I was, too. I think our next move is to get Carla on the phone," Kelsey said.

"You took the words right out of my mouth."

Chapter 45

Tuesday, September 27, 2022

J osh woke up thinking about his last date with Kelsey. He had never connected with any girl like he did with her, and it was refreshing. His ex-girlfriend back in Seattle had been high-maintenance and picky, while Kelsey was just the opposite.

As he picked his phone up to text Kelsey, he saw a notification from a blocked number.

GO BACK TO SEATTLE. THERE'S NOTHING HERE FOR YOU.

Chapter 46

Tuesday, September 27, 2022

There was a knock on the cabin door, and Tina assumed it was Tommy. It was lunchtime after all. He didn't call out to her like he normally did, so she peeked out the window. A man in a black jacket with an Oakview Police Department patch on the shoulder stood on the cabin porch. It wasn't Chief James or Detective Hart. Tentatively, she opened the door.

"Hey, Tina? I'm Officer Klein, and I've been sent to move you to another location," the officer said. "Please pack up your personal belongings. I'll be waiting here for you."

Tina nodded but thought to herself, *Moving locations? Why?*

She packed up her things and slid her phone into her back pocket. She would text Kelsey on the road. As she exited the cabin, she looked back. Had the cabin been compromised? Had someone other than the guards been watching her?

The officer guided her into the back seat of the police cruiser, hurriedly looking around as he did so. As Tina looked out the window, she noticed none of the guards were in their usual spots. *Where did they go? Did the officer send them home? Did Chief James send them home?*

The officer pulled onto the dirt road away from the cabin and within minutes, they were driving on the main road, south on Highway 1. As they moved farther south, Tina started to worry. *Where was he taking her, and why were they driving farther away from Oakview?*

Chapter 47

Tuesday, September 27, 2022

"Umm, excuse me? Officer? Can you tell me where we're going?" Tina asked, hoping the officer would give her more information but knowing he probably wouldn't.

"Sorry, I can't disclose that information. We're almost there. I'm taking you somewhere safe. Don't worry. You can trust me."

Tina's hands started to get sweaty. *Could she take her phone out and text Kelsey without the officer noticing?* She slid her phone from her pocket, keeping it low and turning the volume off.

in car with officer who says they are moving my location. can u ask your dad what is going on?

Kelsey responded within seconds. *what? why would they be moving u? where are u?*

moving south on 1 past Santa Cruz

calling Dad

In what seemed like an eternity, Kelsey texted her back. *my dad said they didn't send an officer. share your location with me so we can track you. please be careful. xoxo*

Tina's stomach dropped when she saw Kelsey's text. She quickly turned on her location-sharing with Kelsey and slid her phone back into her pocket. *Who is this guy? Does he want to hurt me? Is he involved in my mom's death?* Suddenly, Tina had an idea.

"Hey, excuse me. I don't feel well. I think it's the windy road. I feel like I'm going to be sick. Can you pull over and let me out?"

She coughed a few times and made her best gagging impression. The officer pulled over onto the shoulder. Getting out of the car, he opened her door. Pushing past him, Tina propelled herself from the vehicle and started running, keeping her head down but her eyes up. The sweat dripped into her eyes as she ran as fast as she could. The officer was close behind. Tina felt like she was running forever, surrounded by hills covered in tan and brown grass along the long, snaking road. When the officer caught up to her, he grabbed the back of her shirt and pulled her toward him.

"Hey, stop! Hold on a minute!" he said, breathing heavily.

Pulling out of his grasp, Tina stumbled on a rock and fell, her eyes burning with tears as she scrambled to get up. Her fingers gripped the dirt, and her legs pushed, but she was getting nowhere. He pulled her up off the ground and said, "Stop! I don't want to hurt you. I just want to talk."

"Get away from me!" Tina yelled as she clawed at his face. He turned his head to avoid her flailing arms. Cars were whizzing by on the highway. Any closer, and they would both be roadkill.

"What the fuck? Who are you? I'm not a prisoner!" she screamed, spitting at him.

"Listen, dammit. I just need you to listen. Please. I need to talk to you. I need your help. We're not safe," the officer said as he pulled her up off the ground.

Tina stood and with all of the energy she had left, kicked him hard between his legs. He let go of her and bent over in agony, grabbing at his stomach. Tina gave him a good shove and he stumbled backward. She started to run once again. She didn't dare look back.

Chapter 48

Tuesday, September 27, 2022

Kelsey was frantic as she sped to the police station. She had been at a doctor's appointment ten minutes from Oakview when Tina's urgent text had come through. Chuckie's engine roared as they hit eighty-five miles per hour on the 101, the landscape blurring past. Her knuckles turned white as she gripped the steering wheel, her eyes darting back and forth from the road before her to her mounted cell phone. She was now on the line with Randy, breathlessly relaying live updates on the latest pings from Tina's phone.

"Okay, wait. She's moving north on one now. Passing Red, White, and Blue Beach. Why are they moving in the direction they came from?" Kelsey said as she pulled into the station lot. She heard her dad relay the information to dispatch.

"We've got her. It looks like she's in a brown sedan. A little old lady is driving. Sanchez is right behind her," the dispatcher said to Randy.

Kelsey's phone rang. It was Tina.

"Dad, hang on. I've got Tina calling on the other line. I'm at the front door. Can you have Miriam buzz me in?" Kelsey said as she switched calls. The station door buzzed and Kelsey opened it and ran back to her dad's office.

"Kelsey! I hitched a ride from a lady. She's driving me back to Oakview."

"Thank God you're okay. Do you see the officer behind you? It's Officer Sanchez. He was sent to get you. Have the lady pull over. Stay with me on the line, though."

Kelsey could hear Tina thank the lady and get out of the vehicle.

"We've got her, sir. She's safe and secure. We're bringing her back to you," Sanchez said.

Randy looked relieved as he said, "Great job, Sanchez. I'll see you in a few. Did you get the name of the lady who picked her up?"

"Yes, sir. I did. I wrote it down in my notepad with her phone number."

"Excellent work. I'll call her myself and express my gratitude," Randy said. "Let's get Tina back to the station in one piece."

Randy paced back and forth in his office, his adrenaline lingering. How could one of his own betray him like this?

Chapter 49

Tuesday, September 27, 2022

Tina walked into the station escorted by Officer Sanchez, her leggings covered in dirt with a large tear that ran across one knee. Kelsey ran over to hug her, and Tina squeezed her hard. They sat in Randy's office as Officer Sanchez gave Randy an oral report. They still needed to find out who the mystery officer was. Somehow, the officer either disabled or blocked the transmission of the police car's GPS.

"Do you remember what the officer looked like?" Randy asked as he placed a tape recorder in front of Tina.

"He was tall with dark brown hair. I didn't see his eye color. And he was maybe in his late twenties?" Tina said, trying to recollect what happened.

"Did he have any moles, tattoos, or other markings that could distinguish him?"

"He had a mustache. It was like one of those handlebar-looking ones," Tina said.

Randy sat, thinking for a minute. There were precisely three officers in the department who could fit this description. The mustache narrowed it down.

"Anything else? Anything he said that sounded suspicious?"

"Not that I can remember. Oh, he introduced himself as Officer Klein. Klein or Stein. No, it was Klein," said Tina. "Is that a real officer? Sorry, I don't have more to go on. I wasn't even sure if he was a real police officer, but he had the Oakview patch on his jacket. None of the guards were outside when we left."

"Odd. We don't have a Klein on the force," Randy said, shaking his head.

Chapter 50

Tuesday, September 27, 2022

After a long day at the gym, Saffron settled in with some warm cocoa and a book. She had signed up three new members and had created a new membership marketing campaign. Her three-bedroom house, nestled in the cozy Burlingame Hills, was the perfect location—far enough from the bustling city to not hear traffic but close enough to run down the hill to the store in only a few minutes. She was daydreaming about creating a home office in her third bedroom. As she grabbed her phone to log onto Pinterest for ideas, it rang.

"Hey, Kelsey, what's up?" Saffron said.

"Hey, Saff. Are you busy?"

"No, not at all. I just got home from the gym. Why? What's up?"

"Do you think Tina and I can come hide out at your place for a bit? I can explain when I see you."

"Tina? Yes, of course. Come over," Saffron said.

***

Ten minutes later, Kelsey and Tina arrived at Saffron's house. The house was warm and smelled of vanilla.

"Thanks for letting us come here, Saff. I know it's short notice. I didn't think taking her to my place would be safe," Kelsey said as she took her coat off.

Saffron headed to the kitchen and walked out with a tray holding three mugs of hot cocoa with little marshmallows. Tina and Kelsey each took a mug and blew on the cocoa before taking small sips.

"This is so good, Saffron," Tina said, shivering the cold from her bones. "Thank you."

"So, what's going on?" Saffron asked.

Tina told them after she arrived at the station from her grandparents' house, the police asked her what she wanted to do. They advised her that staying hidden and out of public view was in her best interest since her mom's case was still open. They brought her to a cabin close by where she could hear the sound of water on the shore. The same four security guards patrolled the area. She told them about Tommy who brought her food during the guards' food runs.

Tina continued, "Then, today, an officer I had never seen before knocked on my door and said the police were moving me to another location. I wasn't sure what was going on. My dad had already turned himself in, so who were they hiding me from? And why switch locations? I went with him, but I could see no other officers or security guards around on the way out. I figured maybe he had sent the security guards home. Once he started driving, it seemed like he was driving really far. I got scared and started thinking that maybe he wasn't legit. That's when I texted Kelsey."

Tina and Kelsey took turns telling Saffron what happened after that and about Tina's dramatic getaway. When they finished, Tina said, "This has been the craziest two weeks. I mean, you can't make this stuff up. I still can't believe my mom is gone. It all seems like a bad dream."

The trio sat in silence as they figured out what to do next. Kelsey volunteered to go to Anna and Tina's house to grab some clothes for Tina. Saffron suggested ordering takeout from the new Indian restaurant down the street. Saffron placed their order—tandoori paneer, butter chicken, spiced cauliflower, and steamed vegetables.

Kelsey took the back road down to Oakview—better safe than sorry. While driving, she called her dad to get an update on whether Detective Hart was able to interview Carla. The good news was that Oakview PD was able to fly Carla in and would interview her on Friday. Kelsey received some satisfaction knowing Carla might be able to shed some light on this family with all the secrets.

Chapter 51

Tuesday, September 27, 2022

*H*_{i Kelsey! interested in dinner this Friday? my partner told} me about a new hibachi restaurant.

Kelsey looked at her phone and felt the butterflies swarm around in her stomach. She hadn't had a steady boyfriend since college. She enjoyed spending time with Josh and felt their relationship had gotten off to a good start. Kelsey relayed the message to Saffron and Tina.

"He's one of the Oakview officers. He's a rookie who's been with the Oakview force for just over a month. We've been out on a couple of dates, and I like him," explained Kelsey.

"What's he like?" Tina asked.

Kelsey and Saffron took turns describing Josh: handsome, dark features, and worked with Randy. Tina nodded with approval, happy her sister found someone she liked being with. Tina didn't remember Kelsey ever going on a date in the five years they had been training. For a while, she thought Kelsey and Justin would become an item, but Kelsey had put him in the friend zone for reasons unknown.

Kelsey texted Josh back.

sure! that sounds good. I get off work 5:30 that day.

The three little dots twinkled on the screen for a few seconds.

Great! Does 7 work? I can come pick u up at your place.

Kelsey responded with a thumbs-up emoji.

Chapter 52

Wednesday, September 28, 2022

From: Randy James <u>randy.james@oakviewpd.gov</u>

To: Kelsey James kelsey@kelseyjames.com

Subject: Fwd: Interview with Carla

Transcript from Detective Lyle Hart's interview with Carla Sims (neé Eriksen)

Detective Hart: Hi, Carla. Thanks so much for coming in on such short notice.

Carla: Of course. I can't believe Anna is dead. [sniffles]

Detective Hart: I'm sure hearing that news was hard for you. We're trying to get to the bottom of this and bring the killer to justice. Any information you share with us today will be used for that, okay?

Carla: [nods] Okay. I want that, too.

Detective Hart: Great. When was the last time you spoke to Anna? Either by phone or in person? Carla: It must have been right after our senior year of high school. We graduated and went our separate ways. I went to school in Las Vegas, and Anna stayed here.

Detective Hart: I see. Do you come to visit your brother Leo often?

Carla: No, not really. During the holidays, he and Mae sometimes fly out to visit us. They don't have children, so it's easier for them to come to us.

Detective Hart: Understandable. Do you speak to your brother often?

Carla: Umm, not too much. Not because we don't like one another. We were very close growing up. Anna was like a little sister to him. We have our own lives now and don't live close, so we don't talk much. Our dad is in a nursing home here in the Bay Area. He has dementia, so sometimes we have to talk about him. It's not a pleasant topic for either of us.

Detective Hart: I understand. And I'm sorry to hear about your father.

Carla: Don't be. Our dad has always been a total asshole and womanizer for as long as I can remember. The dementia has made him even meaner.

Detective Hart: I see. Can you tell me more about him and what it was like growing up with a

father like that?

Carla: Sure, no problem. I can tell you about his shortcomings for days. As I said, he was not a nice man. He would constantly berate Leo even though Leo was a good kid. That's probably why Leo was so protective of Anna and me. He knew my dad was a bad man. Leo hates him more than anybody. My dad was in and out of jail for embezzlement and various degrees of fraud. I was too little to know the details. Oh, and did I mention he was a womanizer? Yes, that's probably what he is the most guilty of. He was sick in the head. He sure made a lot of money after he got out of prison, though. He struck it rich, the bastard. He ended up buying some stock that made him millions.

Detective Hart: Interesting, I see. And I'm sure you know about the baby that Anna had during sophomore year.

Carla: [long pause] Sure. I mean, I don't really know about it. I wasn't there when she was pregnant. She just stopped coming to school one day and cut everyone off. She wouldn't even answer my calls.

Detective Hart: And how did you feel about that?

Carla: It hurt. It hurt a lot. She was my best friend. My family took care of her when hers neglected her. If she was in trouble, we would have helped her. It didn't make sense for her to cut us off, but I guess when I look back at it, she was probably scared and embarrassed, too.

Detective Hart: Who do you think the father is?

Carla: I have no idea. As far as I know, she wasn't dating anyone at the time, but we were partying a lot. It could have been a one-night stand. The rumor at the time was that the father was my brother Leo. I think people just made that up because she was so close to our family. Leo loved her, but more like a little sister. I can't imagine her sleeping with him. She liked more of the jock type. She liked football players. Back in the day, my brother was actually scrawny. Tall, but not the big buffed guy you see today.

Detective Hart: When was the next time you saw Anna?

Carla: I think she came back either junior or senior year. I didn't talk to her much after she ghosted me. Just pleasantries like hi, bye, how are you. Small talk.

Detective Hart: Is your mother still with us?

Carla: My mom died several years ago of colon cancer. She and my dad stayed married all those years, even though it was not a happy marriage. She stuck by him through everything.

Detective Hart: Sorry to hear about your mom. You said your dad is at an assisted living facility here in the Bay?

Carla: Yes, right here in Oakview, where they have nurses on staff 24-7. It's expensive, but my dad can afford it. He has plenty of money.

Detective Hart: I know Leo spoke to Anna a lot. They were close. Have you talked to him about any of this?

Carla: Yeah, he called me after she was murdered. I couldn't believe it. He said he felt like his heart had been broken in two. He was distraught.

Detective Hart: Did he say who he thought could have done it?

Carla: No. He said it seemed like a random occurrence—like a robbery gone wrong.

Detective Hart: Is there any speculation about whether it could have been something to do with her work or someone she had been seeing?

Carla: No, nothing like that. Nothing at all.

[End of interview.]

Chapter 53

T he sun was out and birds could be heard chirping from the treetops. Justin strolled into Fox Fitness ready to start his training sessions, refreshed after a quick visit to see his parents in Austin. There was nothing like your mama's home-cooked food. While there, he caught up with his friend Travis over burgers and beer at the Workhorse Bar.

Kelsey ran up to Justin and gave him a big bear hug, asking him questions about his trip. Justin was excited to know what happened while he was gone. Kelsey quickly filled Justin in on the unknown police officer who kidnapped Tina and her daring escape. She also told him a little about Carla's interview but before she could tell him everything, Favian walked in for his session.

Favian's routine today was back and biceps, and he loaded the lat pulldown machine, the most incorrectly used machine in the gym. Kelsey was constantly helping gym members with their form. After tiring out Favian's muscles, they ended with the infamous burpees.

Lunchtime arrived, and Justin ran over to Kelsey, heading for her at full speed like the Tasmanian devil. He laughed as she dodged him and giggled. They decided to get some Cane's fried chicken and Texas Toast for lunch while Saffron watched Finley. On the way, they discussed Tina's kidnapping.

Chapter 54

Thursday, September 29, 2022

J ustin finished his sessions at 4:30 p.m. and agreed to take
Finley back to his place so Kelsey could stay to complete her
quad and glute workout—squats, leg extensions, and Bulgarian
split squats. She would feel it tomorrow. After her workout,
she texted Justin asking him what he wanted for dinner. They
agreed on salads and flatbreads from Stafford's Deli, a small
gourmet grocery store a mile and a half from the gym.

The aroma of spiced meats, cheeses, and pepperoncini hit her
as Kelsey entered Stafford's. She headed straight to the counter
to order their food, her mouth-watering. Gino, the owner, was
manning the register and greeted her with a friendly hello.

"Ciao, Bella! How are we doing today, Miss Kelsey?" he
asked.

"Hi, Gino! *We* are starving!" Kelsey said, laughing, "It smells
wonderful in here."

"I take it you are ordering food for you and Mr. Justin. Am I
right?"

"Right, you are! We'll have our usual—a large Caesar with chicken, dressing on the side, Italian sausage and arugula flatbread for Justin, and the ahi flatbread for me."

"Coming right up!"

Kelsey sat down at a bistro table and observed the black-and-white framed photos on the deli wall. There was an autographed photo of Frank Sinatra and another of a group of men sitting in a diner booth. The men were laughing and holding up steins of beer in celebration.

"Excuse me," a woman in her mid to late forties with short black hair said, catching Kelsey off guard. "You're Kelsey, correct?"

"I am," Kelsey said. "Do I know you?"

"You train my niece, Tina. I'm Mae. Mae Eriksen. My husband tells me you're also the chief of police's daughter and that you asked him questions about my sister-in-law."

"Yes, that's correct. Leo agreed to meet with me. We're both trying to learn more about what happened to Anna," Kelsey answered, unsure of where this was going.

"I'm not sure why you've decided to stick your nose into our family business, but I would rather you not. We're a very private family. I don't know what my idiot husband was thinking when he agreed to meet with you. I want you to stay out of our family's personal matters and mind your own business. We will handle this." And with that, she stomped off before Kelsey could react.

Chapter 55

K elsey arrived at Justin's place, talking a mile a minute. Justin began to unwrap the food, listening carefully to every detail Kelsey told him about the run-in.

"Can you believe that?" Kelsey said when she finished the story.

"Do you think she's the one who's been sending you the texts? It sure wouldn't be smart of her to be threatening the police chief's daughter," Justin said.

"Maybe. Or maybe she's just being protective over her family. Nick is innocent. Tina is kidnapped by her uncle and then a cop? Who might not even be a cop? Who would kill Anna? And what is up with the stick up Mae's butt?" Kelsey thought out loud. "I'm going to call Tina and see if her aunt and uncle have said anything to her about the baby her mom gave up."

Kelsey dialed and Tina picked up on the second ring.

"Hi, Kelsey!"

"Hi! I wanted to ask you something. I'm going down the rabbit hole here, but do you know if your Aunt Mae or Uncle

Leo have any information about the baby your mom had when she was younger?"

There was a slight pause, and then Tina replied, "Actually, it's interesting that you ask. Mae is the executor of my mom's will. When I was at my grandparents' house, she kept asking me questions about the baby. I told her my mom never talked about it. Just that it was a boy and that he was adopted. Mae wouldn't stop bugging me about it. When I asked her why she wanted to know, she said that my mom left him something in the will. Sorry, Kelsey. I wish I could be more help. Do you think the baby has something to do with my mom's murder?"

"I'm not sure. I'm still trying to put the pieces of the puzzle together. What was she trying to find out?"

"My aunt said she was trying to find out who the father was."

"Interesting," Kelsey said, tapping her finger to her chin as she tried to figure out why Mae would need to know this information.

"What if Mae thought the father found out Anna put his kid up for adoption so he killed her?" Justin cut in.

"But why now?" Kelsey said.

"I can ask Mae and see if she tells me more. What if I tell her I want to help her in finding the father?" Tina said.

"That's a great idea. Try to play innocent. For example, since your mom died, say you've been thinking about how you have a sibling out there, and you'd like to find him. See how she reacts."

"Good idea."

"And Tina?"

"Yeah?"

"Be careful. We don't want anyone to figure out where you are. It's still not safe."

Chapter 56

Friday, September 30, 2022

"Hi, Auntie!" Tina said as she tried to remember what to say and what not to say to Mae.

"Hi, honey. How are you holding up? Is there anything Leo and I can help with?" Mae said, sounding concerned.

"Actually, there is. Remember how you were asking me about the father of my mom's baby?" Tina said and could hear Mae gasp quietly on the other end.

"Yes. Did you find out, Tina? Do you know who the father is?"

"No, but I thought I could help you in finding out. I mean, after all, he is my brother."

"Oh, Tina, I am so happy to hear you say that. Yes, dear. Let's get together for a coffee tomorrow. I have a lunch date at one, so let's meet at Café Blanco at 12:15, yes?"

"Sure, Auntie. I'll see you tomorrow."

Chapter 57

K elsey rushed home from the gym and threw her gym bag down in her front entryway. How had she almost forgotten about her date with Josh? She took Finley out for a quick bathroom break and filled his kibble and water bowls. Looking at the time, she had fifteen minutes to shower and get ready before Josh arrived. The doorbell rang just as she was putting her shoes on.

"Hi!" she said, opening the door. Josh held a gorgeous bouquet of wildflowers in one hand, his other hand behind his back. He wore gray wool dress pants, dress shoes, and a white button-down shirt. "Are those for me?"

Josh answered, "I thought you might like them. You look very pretty." He revealed a bottle of zinfandel reserve from a local winery in his other hand. "Oh, I also brought this. For later, maybe."

Kelsey blushed and thanked him. Her new little black dress was both sexy and flirty, with a skinny red patent leather belt for a splash of color. She paired them with a pair of open-toed black suede platforms Saffron told her she had to buy on their last shopping trip.

"I love that winery!" Kelsey gasped excitedly. "That's some expensive stuff, Mr. DeLuca."

Kelsey unwrapped the bouquet and neatly placed the flowers in a vase with water. She put the bottle of wine in the refrigerator. Many people didn't know you could chill a good red wine to reveal nuances you might not get with a room-temperature bottle.

Kelsey laughed as she sank into Josh's Camaro. Josh looked at her, confused.

"I'm so used to being up high in Chuckie, I forgot what it was like to sit in a car! I feel like I'm sitting on the ground."

Josh laughed and replied, "I get it. I feel the same way about trucks. I feel like I'm floating above the Earth."

As they were driving, they discovered they liked the same eclectic mix of songs. From country ballads to sing-along pop, they laughed as Vanessa Carlton's song "A Thousand Miles" came on and they recalled Terry Crews singing the song in *White Chicks*. Singing along and doing the quick head movements Terry's character did in the movie, they laughed so hard that Kelsey snorted! This made Josh laugh even harder and a few tears escaped the corner of his eyes. He wiped them away and laughed even harder, trying to catch his breath.

"I haven't laughed that hard in a long time," he said. "That was awesome." Josh turned to smile at Kelsey and reached over to hold her hand. Kelsey felt little tingles going through her body. He reached to change the radio station and "Country

Roads" came on. Once again, they sang along in perfect sync but not so much in perfect harmony.

"I love that song," he said. "It reminds me of when I was a kid. Sometimes, my dad would take me on a fishing trip. We would drive on this long road, and it seemed like no one else was on it except us. We would fish for the day in a little boat. My dad would pack sandwiches for us, beer for himself, and sodas for me. My mom always felt it was important for us to spend one-on-one time with them even though they were so busy at the restaurant. Good times."

They arrived at the restaurant—Sapporo Hibachi and Sushi. The lighting was dim, and the decor was beautiful—banners with Japanese writing and little red lanterns. The server, dressed in a kimono and little wood sandals, seated them at a large table near the back window.

"Any special occasion tonight?" the server asked with a polite smile.

"It's my birthday today," Josh said.

"Wonderful," the server replied, placing their menus in front of them. She told them the specials of the night: Japanese Curry Chicken and a Dragon Fire Roll.

"It's your birthday? Why didn't you tell me?" Kelsey said, now horrified she didn't get him anything.

Josh shrugged. "I don't know. Don't worry. It's not that big a deal. Plus, I never told you when my birthday was." He changed the subject. "This place is nice. It looks like my patrol partner Allen came through with his promise of a romantic restaurant. He said he took his wife here for their anniversary and she loved it."

"I can see why. I love the decor. It looks like each table has different patterned lanterns hanging above them. I wish I knew what the banners said."

"I love the mural of the monkeys, too," he said. Kelsey turned around to see a large wall-sized mural of monkeys with a snow-covered backdrop.

"That is something. It's beautiful."

"Sorry, so what were we talking about? I got distracted by the cool ambiance in here," Josh said, apologizing. "Oh, movies, that's right. I watched my little sister Chelsea a lot growing up and I usually got stuck watching kid movies and chick flicks. She likes that movie where the girls are twins, and they switch bodies. What was that one called?"

"*The Parent Trap*. You know the Lindsay Lohan version is a remake, right?" Kelsey said, turning to look at him.

"Really? When was the old one made?"

"I think it was in the 1960s or something. I watched it with my mom when I was a kid. It was pretty good for its time.

"I'll have to tell Chelsea. I'm sure she'd be down to see that version. She was obsessed with the new one. She would come home from school every day and pop the DVD in to watch it while she had her afterschool snack."

"That's so cute that you spent so much time with your sister growing up. It's nice to have a sibling you get along with."

"It is. I talk to her on the phone almost every day. She's a junior in high school this year, so she's trying to figure out what she wants to do. It's either college applications or work at the restaurant. My parents have always believed in letting us make our own life decisions. Although, I think they would love for

Chelsea to take over the family business. She works part time at the restaurant during the school year and the summer, so she knows the ins and outs of running the place. She's a smart girl. Straight As and the captain of her lacrosse team."

"She sounds like she would be fun to be around. And that's cool that your parents are not all strict."

"Yeah, even though they weren't home most of the time, they made sure we had everything we needed." Josh looked a little sad as he recalled his childhood.

"Can I ask you something? It's something kind of personal. You don't have to answer if you don't want to."

"Sure. Ask away," Josh said and a smile returned to his face.

"Have you ever thought of looking up your biological parents?" Kelsey asked.

"That's funny you ask. It's the real reason I put in for a transfer down here. I wanted to meet my biological parents to see what they're like."

The server came over with glasses of ice water, and they order a bottle of a light, crisp sauvignon blanc, and the surf and turf. Kelsey added a lemon drop roll to the order.

"So, did you find them?" Kelsey asked.

"I found out my mother passed away during childbirth. I can't seem to find out where she's buried, though. Maybe she was cremated? I'm still doing some detective work trying to figure out who my father is," Josh said.

"I'm so sorry to hear about your mom. Do you know if she had any siblings?"

"As far as I know, she didn't," Josh said, taking a sip of wine.

After dinner, the server brought Josh's birthday sundae to the table—a scoop of matcha ice cream with a candle on top and a scoop of vanilla for Kelsey. The server smiled, and Josh and Kelsey squeezed close as she took their picture. She brought the picture to them in a cardboard frame with the restaurant's name. Kelsey and Josh watched as the Polaroid picture developed, as if by magic. Kelsey took her phone out to snap a photo of it so Josh could take the original home.

"Are you sure you don't want to keep this one?" Josh offered.

"No! It's your birthday, silly! You keep it."

After stuffing themselves with sushi, they drove back to Kelsey's place and she invited Josh in for a drink.

"That bottle of wine you brought over isn't going to drink itself," Kelsey laughed as they approached her front door.

Finley greeted them at the front door and Kelsey said, "I'm going to take Fin out for a quick pee. The wine glasses are in the top cabinet to the left of the stove." Josh nodded and headed to the kitchen. Kelsey slipped out of her heels and into a pair of sneakers to take Fin out.

The warmth of the red wine set in as Kelsey and Josh sank into the couch side by side. The wine was on the dry side but had velvety red fruit like plums and raspberries. Kelsey got up to go to the kitchen and brought back a bar of dark chocolate. She broke two pieces off, handing Josh one. They both take a bite and then a sip of wine.

"That makes the flavors of the wine stand out. And I like it chilled like this," Josh said, holding his glass up.

Kelsey closed her eyes to savor the velvety chocolate on her tongue and the tannins of the wine. Josh leaned over and gently kissed her, his hand running through her soft brown hair. She kissed him back, a little harder. He took her wine glass and set it down on the table. Leaning in toward her, their kisses became more intense. His cologne was clean yet woodsy, and Kelsey breathed him in. As she pulled him in toward her, she lay down on the couch with him on top and slowly let her hands wander up under the back of his shirt. His skin was smooth and warm, just like his kisses.

"Bedroom?" Kelsey whispered.

He looked at her, picking his head up and looking her in the eye. "If you want this. I don't want to pressure you into anything."

She pulled him back down to kiss him and whispered, "I do. I want this." Picking her up, he walked into the bedroom and closed the door behind him.

Chapter 58

Saturday, October 1, 2022

K elsey and Tina arrived at the café to meet with Mae fifteen minutes early. As the server put Kelsey's decaf iced coffee on the table, the tiny ding of the front doorbell went off. Mae walked in with a gentle smile, wearing a pink tweed jacket, matching pencil skirt, frilly blouse, and very high nude-colored heels. She also had a multitude of delicate bracelets on each wrist, along with a large diamond on her left ring finger. Her makeup was flawless, each hair perfectly in place.

Upon seeing Kelsey, Mae's brow furrowed. "Why is she here?" she asked Tina.

"I don't go anywhere alone nowadays. Surely you understand why, Auntie," Tina said.

"Oh, well. Fine then. That's your choice. Although I would be careful who you discuss any of this with. This is no one's business but our own family." Aunt Mae sighed and sat down across from Tina who nodded at her aunt in acknowledgement.

"So, any news on the topic of your brother's father? Think hard, Tina. Did your mother ever tell you about her past boyfriends?" Mae grilled Tina.

"I've been trying to remember if my mom ever spoke about people from her past but I can't recall anything. I don't even remember her talking about girl friends she was close to. Everything I knew about my mom had to do with our family."

Mae sat, pondering for a minute, then said, "Can you both keep a secret?"

Kelsey and Tina nodded, excited to hear what Mae had to say.

"I've always thought the baby was Leo's."

"What? Why?" Tina gasped. "Is that why you want to find the baby? To see if Uncle Leo is the father?"

"Are you sure your mother didn't tell you anything else about the baby? Maybe she mentioned an ex-boyfriend who could be the father?" Mae asked, ignoring Tina's questions.

"No, nothing. I'm sure."

"Hmm, I spoke with your father and he didn't know anything either. So secretive, that mother of yours.," Mae said and she could see Tina's face drop. "Oh, honey. I'm sorry. Don't mind me. I'm just a bit buggered about it because your mother left me with the work of having to track this kid down because she didn't think to put his address in her will. Well, if you think of anything, let me know."

And with that, Mae stood up, slinging her purse over her shoulder, keys in hand.

"Oh, another thing. Auntie, could you make me a copy of my mom's will? Just so I can look over it," Tina asked.

"Yes, I'll make a copy for you and send it certified. Where should I have it delivered?

The house?" Mae asked.

"Could you have it sent to Fox Fitness on Fifth? Saffron takes care of the mail, and I'll tell her to be on the lookout for it."

"Will do," Mae said, blowing Tina a kiss. "Bye now."

"Bye, Auntie," Tina said and she and Kelsey watched as Mae strutted out the front door.

"Isn't that crazy? She thinks Leo might be the kid's dad," Kelsey said.

"I wonder if there's truth behind it, though. Mae can be very dramatic. That's what makes her a good attorney. But who knows? My mom and Leo were very close."

"That was a smart move to get a copy of your mom's will. I wonder if it has your brother's name in it."

"Good point. Maybe we can track him down before Mae does." Tina added.

Chapter 59

Saturday, October 1, 2022

With Finley in tow, Kelsey arrived at Saffron's house for a girls' night. She was juggling three grocery bags and her duffle bag. Finley darted to his toy box and settled on a multicolored rope toy. Tina and Charlie were standing at the counter sipping on glasses of wine. They ran over to help Kelsey with the bags.

"Ooh, I don't remember the last time I had strawberry short-cake. This is such a good idea!" Tina said as she took out a carton of strawberries, a small carton of heavy whipping cream, and a package of ladyfingers. "Strawberries are my favorite fruit."

"Mine too!" Kelsey said.

"Well, you two are sisters. I wonder how many other things you have in common," Saffron said.

"We should make a list of favorites," Tina said. "Not just me and Kelsey, but all of us. It would be fun to know our likes and dislikes."

"That would make a fun drinking game!" Kelsey said.

Saffron laid out a platter of chips, salsa, and guacamole for the girls to munch on.

"So, how has living with Saffron been, Tina? This house is amazing," Charlie asked while taking in and appreciating Saffron's decorating skills.

"I'm so grateful for Saffron opening her place to me. I'm trying to be a good houseguest."

She looked over at Saffron who said, "You're the best houseguest. And you're welcome to stay for as long as you want. My house has never been cleaner. I come home from work and the place is spotless! I could get used to this."

"Speaking of houseguests, I heard someone had a sleepover last night," Charlie said, laughing.

"Oh, let me guess. Saffron told you about Josh spending the night. It was nice," Kelsey said, not surprised at how quickly the word spread.She had texted Saffron that morning to announce the exciting news that she and Josh were official.

"Just nice?" Charlie said with a mischievous grin.

"Okay, girls! Let's get these drinks started! Kelsey, your spritzers sound perfect to start off with. Who wants white, who wants red?" Saffron asked, holding four chilled stemless wine glasses.

They started with the white wine, a sauvignon blanc. Kelsey paired hers with the Limonata soda. The bubbles were fun, and the fruitiness of the soda made it feel like you weren't drinking alcohol. Tina also tried the Limonata and made a face because it was a little tart. She poured some of the blood orange soda into her cocktail, took a sip, and said, "Oh, yeah, that's much better." After tasting Kelsey's drink, Saffron and Charlie decide on Pompelmo, the grapefruit soda, both saying it might be the winner paired with the sauvignon blanc.

"Okay, so back to Kelsey and her sleepover," Saffron said, and Charlie and Tina's ears perked up.

"It was good. It was better than good. He's one of those guys who has a really good body with a lot of muscle but not too much where they're bulging out everywhere."

"Geez, Kelsey, you really know how to create a fantasy. So sexy." Saffron rolled her eyes and everyone laughed. "So, tell us the good stuff. Like is he a good kisser? Is he selfish or does he like to take care of you first?"

"Hey, hey!" Kelsey put her hands over Tina's ears, "Not in front of my little sister!" All three girls burst into laughter and Tina laughed so hard she snorted. "I swear, you think I'm like ten years old, Kelsey!" she said. "Remember, I can bench more than you."

"Oooooh!!!" said Saffron and Charlie in unison.

"Yeah, yeah, okay, you're right," Kelsey said.

"Josh is so good-looking, though. And he's always polite at the gym. He's not a weight hog or one of those guys who grunts with every rep," Charlie said.

"Plus, he doesn't wear HOKAs so that's major points in his book," added Kelsey.

Saffron removed some pigs in a blanket from the oven and plated them. Taking a little dish out, she poured barbecue sauce for dipping.

"I want to see what he looks like. I feel like I haven't been to the gym in forever," Tina said.

Then, Kelsey remembered the picture from dinner the other night. She pulled her phone out and told them about the hibachi restaurant and how Josh paid even though it was his birthday. Opening her photo roll, she handed the phone to Tina. Saffron and Charlie huddled around her to look. Tina's face turned as white as a ghost, and her hand flew up to her mouth as she gasped.

"Tina, what's wrong?" Kelsey asked she placed her hand on Tina's back.

"That's him, Kelsey," she said with wide eyes. "That's the cop who took me from the cabin. He's the one I ran away from. He had a mustache when I met him, but I'm sure that's him."

"Are you sure?" Charlie asked. "Maybe it's just someone who looks like him."

"Yeah, I've never seen Josh with a mustache. He was just at the gym the other day," Saffron said.

"I'm one hundred percent sure that's him. I remember him looking down at me when I was on the ground," Tina said in disbelief, her heart racing. She zoomed in on the photo and nodded.

"We need to get to the bottom of this. I'm not okay with my boyfriend hurting my sister. Do you remember what he said to you while you were trying to escape?"

"He said he wanted to talk to me and something about not being safe."

"Who's not safe? You?"

"I guess. He seemed like he was panicking. When we were in the car, I could tell he was sweating, but he kept it cool when he spoke. It wasn't until I tried to run that he became gruff. What do you think he wants, Kelsey?"

"I don't know, but I'm going to find out, okay? There has to be something he either needed to tell you or ask you, or something, you know? What could it be? Does Josh know something about your mom's murder?" Kelsey said, tapping her fingers to her chin, deep in thought. "In the meantime, stay safe here at Saffron's and don't open the door for anyone but the people in this room. And Justin, of course. And my dad. Our dad."

Tina nodded, and they devised a safety and emergency plan. Kelsey ensured that all important phone numbers were programmed in Tina's phone and written down on a notepad next to Saffron's landline.

They tried to make the best of the rest of the night after finding out the shocking news of Josh's possible villain status. Saffron made some samosas filled with peas and potatoes and others with chicken in them, and the girls devoured them while attempting to play a game of Clue. They also played the "list your favorites" game Tina suggested, and it turned out they all listed tacos as their favorite food. Well, who *doesn't* like tacos? Charlie found the movie *Clueless* on a streaming service, and they watched it because Saffron had never seen it before. By the end of the movie, she was making Ws with her fingers and quoting the movie.

Suddenly, Tina grabbed Kelsey's arm and pulled her aside. Everyone stopped laughing.

"Kels, I remember," she slurred. "I remember what said... what Josh..."

"You remember what Josh said?" Kelsey said, knowing Tina's response should probably be taken with a grain of salt since she was pretty drunk.

"He said *weee*. *We* are in danger. And he said he needed my help." She stumbled and Kelsey guided her over to the couch.

"You're sure? He said, 'We're in danger.' Did he say plural? Like you and him?" "Mmm hmm." Tina slumped over onto Kelsey's shoulder and passed out.

"Oh, man," said Charlie, who was starting to sober up.

Why would Josh think he *and* Tina were in danger? And who was Josh deLuca?

Chapter 60

Sunday, October 2, 2022

K elsey and Finley left Saffron's place at ten a.m. Before leaving, Kelsey reassured Tina they would get to the bottom of the whole Josh thing. Kelsey pulled into her parents' driveway with Justin pulling up right behind her in his black GMC Sierra a few seconds later.

As Kelsey explained the events of the previous night to Justin, his jaw dropped in surprise. "We've got to tell your dad," he told Kelsey.

Randy and Brian sat at the kitchen table, and Joanna stood at the stove stirring something. Finley trotted over to Brian, who picked him up and put him on the kitchen chair next to his, scooting it close. Brian scratched Finley on the top of his head, and Fin put his paws and head down on Brian's leg.

"Hey, Dad, I have a question for you," Kelsey said.

"Sure thing. What's up, sweetie?" Randy said as he put his newspaper down.

"So, you know how Josh is from Seattle but was born here?"

"Yes. He asked for a transfer down here a few months ago. When something opened up he moved down and started work right away. Why do you ask?"

"Did you ever ask him why he applied to transfer down here?"

"As a matter of fact, yes. I'm sure Josh told you he's adopted, right? He wanted to find his biological parents and meet them."

"Mmm hmm. That's what he told me, too. Has he said anything about what he's found out? He was a little secretive when I asked him."

"You know, I never followed up with him about that."

"Dad, I think Josh is Anna's baby. What's weird is that he told me that his mother died during childbirth. Things aren't adding up. What I do know is that he was the officer who kidnapped Tina. She identified him in a photo we took at dinner the other night. So he must be involved somehow."

Randy's brow furrowed and he contemplated the new information.

"What if Josh *is* the kid who Anna gave up for adoption when she was fifteen?" Justin said.

"Drunk Tina said he told her they were in danger so something is going on. Josh knows something," Kelsey said.

At this point, even Brian was listening, and Joanna jumped at the stove exclaiming, "Oops! I was listening and I burned the first batch of crepes."

"I mean, it's possible," Randy said. "And now that you mention it, he never said whether or not he got to meet his parents."

Randy tapped his chin, deep in thought.

"Don't say it, Dad. I already thought the same thing. There's no way he killed her. And now that we know he came down here to find her, it's even less likely that he would have done it. Why would you find your mom and then kill her? If he was going to do that, he would have come down for a week, gotten the job done, and then gone back home to Seattle. Besides, what would his motive be? That's if Josh is the baby Anna gave up for adoption.

"Do you think you can pull Josh's HR record tomorrow? That way we can see what it says on his birth certificate. Because what if we're completely off and Josh isn't Anna's? Maybe he's just a psycho. I'd like to know if I'm dating a psycho." Kelsey laughed half-heartedly.

"I can. But the birth certificate will most likely show his adoptive parents' names. Not his biological parents." Randy said.

"Ugh. Well, that's a dead end then. We'll have to come up with another way of figuring this out." Kelsey said. "Did Detective Hart interview the Eriksen guy on Friday at the retirement home?"

"They rescheduled the interview for Monday morning. They said when he's well-rested he seems to do better in terms of cognitive ability. Apparently, he didn't sleep well the night before," Randy said.

Joanna started to bring the plates of crepes over. She had bowls and plates of different fillings which made it feel like a breakfast taco bar. She placed a bowl of lingonberry jam, a plate of warmed sliced ham and scrambled eggs, a bowl of shredded cheddar cheese, a jar of Nutella, a jar of peanut butter, a jar of strawberry jelly, and a plate of fresh sliced strawberries on the table.

Brian was already smothering his crepe with Nutella and putting fresh strawberries down the middle. "Yummy!" he said as he licked the Nutella off his fingers.

Kelsey looked at Brian and studied his features. All three of Randy's children had sparkling green eyes. Kelsey and Brian had light brown hair, and Tina had dirty blonde hair.

Josh's hair was dark brown, his eyes blue. She wondered what color hair and eyes Anna had.

Chapter 61

Monday, October 3, 2022

T he sun was shining in the morning, so Kelsey decided to walk to work. She hooked Finley's leash on to his collar, and on their way to the gym, they enjoyed the fabulous fall décor everyone had out. Kelsey caught a whiff of pumpkin spice in the air as they walked past Blake's Coffee Shop. As soon as they entered Fox, all eyes were on the adorable Finley James who dashed over to Saffron. Kelsey strolled over to her first client, Janet, a retired schoolteacher who split her time between babysitting her grandkids and volunteering part time at the SETI, an institute that did cool research on the origin of life on Earth.

As Kelsey guided Janet into her floor exercises, she saw Josh enter the gym. She handed a three-pound dumbbell to Janet during the birddog exercise and tried to stay focused on her client.

"Wow!" Janet said. "Three pounds makes a big difference. It's a lot harder. And here I thought I was getting stronger!"

"You are," Kelsey told her. "Why do you think I added the dumbbell?" They both laughed.

"I love that you push me, Kelsey. I would have never thought to add weight to that one," Janet said, slowly moving into a standing position. "Well, I survived another session with KelseyJames! I will see you Thursday for another wonderful workout."

Kelsey's next session was on video so she grabbed her backpack and hustled into one of the small classrooms. She was a minute late. Josh stopped her as she started to close the classroom door.

"Kelsey!" he said, "Hey, do you have a break this morning? I wanted to ask you something."

"I've got to go into a video session right now, and I'm running late. I'll text you later, okay?"

"Oh, okay," Josh said, looking a little defeated.

Kelsey dialed into her video call, a half-hour session with her client Kimmy. Two minutes before the session ended, Kelsey heard yelling in the gym. *What is that?* She guided Kimmy into another static stretch and quickly sent Saffron a text message, *what's going on?*

Saffron replied immediately, *J&J fighting*, followed by a wide-eyed emoji.

Once her session ended, Kelsey peeked out the classroom door and saw Justin and Josh standing across from each other. Gym members were trying not to stare.

"Dude, what is your problem? If you want to know, ask her. But don't come at me," Justin yelled at Josh as he unloaded the weight rack.

"You know what? You're a dick. All I did was ask you a couple of questions, and you go all psychotic on me. What's your deal? If you like her, then why don't you date her?" Josh replied.

"What are you talking about? Kelsey's my friend, and you're acting like a jealous boyfriend right now. I don't appreciate you coming up to me at work and being a bully. Just because she had to go into her session and couldn't talk to you, you go all nuts," Justin said, shaking his head and walking away.

Josh was standing in the middle of the floor, fuming. Kelsey had to go back out to the gym floor to train Sam. She breathed a sigh of relief when she saw Josh enter the locker room and rush out of the gym, brushing past her and Sam.

"Well, that was exciting for a Monday morning," Sam said.

"I'm not used to all this drama," Kelsey replied.

***

Lunchtime rolled around, and Justin asked, "Hey, you want to go grab lunch?"

"Yeah, sure. I didn't bring Chuckie. Fin and I walked. Maybe we can go grab some hot deli sandwiches at Sam's Italian Deli?" Kelsey said.

"Sounds good. Let me grab my jacket and my wallet and stuff." Justin went into the men's locker room and met Kelsey and Finley outside.

"Saff and Charlie asked if we could pick them up sandwiches, too." Kelsey took a piece of paper out of her pocket and showed it to him.

An uncomfortable silence hovered in the air for the first two blocks as Kelsey thought about how to bring up Justin's encounter with Josh.

"Just so you know, he started it," Justin said.

"I believe you," Kelsey said and kept walking.

"Are you mad?"

"Not at you. It's just that things were going so well with Josh, and then we find out he might be Anna's long-lost kid. And now this. I feel like there's this ominous energy around us. Like we're just waiting for something else bad to happen. What did he say in the beginning?"

"He came up to me and said, 'Hey, why is Kelsey acting so weird?' I said, 'What do you mean?' and he said, 'It's like she doesn't want to talk to me' and I said, 'Well, she's working. She's in a video session, so it's not like she can socialize while she's in there.'"

"That's it?"

"Well, no, and then he started asking questions about you, like about past boyfriends and why we didn't ever date. He asked about your family, and then, oh, get this, he asked if you knew where Tina was. That was what sent me over the edge. It was like he was digging. I think we're on the right track with this investigation, Kels. I think he's hiding something."

"I think you're right." Kelsey stopped walking and so did Justin. She reached up to hug him as he bent down and squeezed her into a tight bear hug.

"I've always got your back, Kelsey Sue," Justin said as he let go of her and smiled with a tear in his eye.

"Aww, did you think I wasn't going to believe *you*, of all people? You know me better than that. Okay, let's stop being all sappy and get these sandwiches. I'm starving!"

Kelsey sat outside with Finley and waited for Justin to get the sandwiches. She took her phone out and saw she had a missed call from her dad.

"Hi, sweetie," Randy answered. "I've got some news. I had to temporarily suspend Josh this morning for tampering with a witness. He admitted the whole thing."

Kelsey sighed and said, "That's probably what he wanted to tell me this morning. He got into a fight with Justin and was being a jerk. I knew he seemed off."

"It's a serious violation," Randy said. "I'm sorry, Kelsey."

"It's not your fault, Dad. It had to be done. Did he tell you why he did it?"

"No. I didn't give him a chance. What he did was unacceptable on all counts. Oh, before I forget, I decided to ask for a copy of his birth certificate from HR anyway."

Kelsey took a deep breath and said, "What did it say?

"Joshua Tyler DeLuca was born on September twentieth, 1990. And sure enough, his adopted parents are listed on it. I did a quick search, and everything seems to match up. They are a happy family who resides in Seattle, Washington with their adopted daughter Chelsea."

It took Kelsey a minute to register the information. "Okay, so he's not a liar. But how do we find out who his birth mother was?"

"I have an idea, Dad. Okay, hear me out. What if I get a piece of Josh's hair, and we do a DNA test to see if he's related to Leo?

Mae seems to think Leo is the baby's father so maybe we can start there. I can get Jason to get hair from Leo," she told him.

"If I were you, I'd let Josh cool down for a few days. Just keep your distance."

"Okay. Bye, Dad."

Justin exited the sandwich shop with two huge bags, grinning from ear to ear. "What in the world did you get? Saff, Charlie, and I only got one sandwich each," Kelsey said to him and peered into the bags.

"I got some potato salad and chips for all of us. Plus, they had that unsweetened peach iced tea you like, so I got you one. And a Gatorade for me."

"Nice, these look great."

"Were you on the phone with your dad?"

Kelsey caught him up on the conversation, and Justin said, "Oh man. Well, at least he's not a liar."

"That's what I said," Kelsey said.

Chapter 62

Monday, October 3, 2022

K elsey's notes:

1. Anna Lorraine Kiel, a.k.a. Anna Lorraine Scott

2. Anna was married to Nick Scott.

3. Anna had an affair with Randy James and got pregnant with Tina

4. Before that, Anna became pregnant when she was fifteen and had baby X (who we think is Josh)

5. Josh was adopted by the DeLucas when he was a baby, and they moved up to Seattle when he was three.

6. The killer was left-handed (probably).

7. Mae wanted to know who the baby was that Anna had; she thought Leo was the father.

8. Leo and Anna were close growing up; Anna's best

friend growing up was Leo's sister, Carla.

9. Carla lives in Las Vegas with her husband and kids. Leo and Carla's father was Sven Eriksen, and he was a womanizer; their mom, Lila, passed away.

Tap. Tap. Tap.

Kelsey's pencil tapped rapidly on her kitchen table. She jumped as her phone rang.

"Hi, Dad. You're at work late," she answered.

"Just tying up some loose ends. The crime has really gone up in Oakview this year. Sheesh!" Randy said and Kelsey could imagine him shaking his head in disbelief.

"Did Hart interview Sven?"

"That's what I was calling about. I haven't listened to the recording yet, but Robert gave me the transcript, so I'll read that to you."

Chapter 63

Detective Hart: Interview with Sven Eriksen

Detective Hart: For the sake of the recording, can I have you state your full name?

Sven: Who are you?

Detective Hart: Mr. Eriksen, I'm Detective Hart. I'm here to ask you a few questions.

Sven: Do I get ice cream if I cooperate?

Detective Hart: Yes, that is what your assistant said. You'll get ice cream if you answer my questions.

Sven: Okay, then. What do you want to know?

Detective Hart: Your full name please?

Sven: Sven Lars Eriksen

Detective Hart: And, Mr. Eriksen, do you remember a young woman named Anna Kiel?

Sven: [pauses] Ahh, Anna, yes. She was a sweet girl. She was the daughter I wish I had had.

Detective Hart: What was your relation to Anna?

Sven: She was my daughter's best friend. She was always at our house. She came from a family that was no good. Her poor mother struggled to make ends meet after her no-good father ran off with some woman. We took care of her.

Detective Hart: And did you spend a lot of time with your daughter and Anna?

Sven: Not more than any other father. I gave my children everything. Do you understand? And did those kids appreciate it? No. They went crying to their mommy. Only Anna appreciated me. She was the sweetest girl—the sweetest—and beautiful too. She was a spitting image of her mother.

Detective Hart: Did you love Anna?

Sven: Of course, I did. She would get me a beer from the fridge when I got home. Say hello. That sort of thing. She cared about how my day went—such a sweet girl. Carla and Leo never thought to do such a thing as to greet me when I came home from work. So, where is Anna nowadays?

Detective Hart: Do you know if your son, Leo, and Anna have ever had sexual relations?

Sven: What is this? Who are you? Are you after my money, too? Get out! Get out of here!

Detective Hart: Sir, calm down. Please calm down. I'm just asking you some questions. I'm not here to take your money.

Sven: Who put you up to this? Leo? Did Leo put you up to this? Where's Anne? Ang. Ang. Oh dear Lord.

Detective Hart: Who's Ang, Sven?

Sven: It was only right, you know. I know I have my faults, but I always make up for them. I make it right. Do you hear me? I make it right. I'm done here. I want my ice cream.

[End of interview]

Chapter 64

Tuesday, October 4, 2022

As she was waiting for Caroline, Kelsey's phone pinged. It was Josh.

hi Kels

i wanted to say i'm sorry about yesterday. idk what i was thinking. can I explain over dinner tomorrow night? i understand if u say no, but there's just some stuff i need to get off my chest. Please. I miss u

"Kelsey, dear! I brought my daughter in with me. She's signing up today and wants to do some training with you. She's at the front desk with Saffron right now. Isn't that exciting?" Kelsey heard Caro's voice coming toward her.

"It is! Audrey, right?" Kelsey said, smiling.

"That's right! You have a good memory. You'll have fun training her. She's a great gal!"

"She must take after her mama," Kelsey said, trying to forget about Josh's text and focus on her job. She would have to get back to him later. The question was, what would she say to him?

Chapter 65

Tuesday, October 4, 2022

On her lunch break, Kelsey waited for Finley to finish his business on a little green bush when she saw Josh pull up in his Camaro.

"Oh, hey!" she said, trying to act natural. "I was going to text you back when I got home, but I had to take Fin out first."

"No worries. I'm glad you were going to text me back. I wasn't sure after the scene I made at the gym yesterday. I just wanted to let you know that it wasn't my intention for that to happen. I'm sure you've heard I've been suspended. I was mad at the way I handled things. And I know I pushed Justin's buttons the wrong way. I need to apologize to him, too."

"Yeah, I've never heard Justin yell like that."

"Do you think you could give me another chance? Maybe we could go out tomorrow night? To talk?"

"I don't know if that's such a good idea," Kelsey said, but the look on Josh's face was so sad and desperate, she started rethinking her response. "Okay, only if we can go to Kyoto's again. Your treat. I have something I want to ask you, too," she said, hoping she wouldn't regret it.

A big smile spread across his face, and he said, "It's a deal. Pick you up at six?"

"That sounds good."

"Okay, then. I'll see you tomorrow. And Kelsey?"

"Yeah?"

"Thanks for the second chance. I promise I won't screw it up this time," he said as he pulled away from the curb. Kelsey stood there watching the Camaro's brake lights as it turned the corner and thought, *He can't be the killer, right? There had to be an explanation for how he was acting. And I'm going to find out what it is.*

Chapter 66

"Are you okay?" Kelsey asked, anxiously tapping her foot under the table. She wanted to know what was going through his head when he kidnapped Tina. And what other secrets was he harboring?

"Let's eat first. I have something that I want to tell you, but I want to tell you on a full stomach. I'm nervous," Josh replied.

The wheels in Kelsey's mind started to spin. Was he going to tell her something she already knew, or did he have a piece of the puzzle none of them had figured out yet? She had a million questions but didn't want to seem too eager.

Kelsey pushed her food around on her plate. Something she never did at Kyoto's.

"I'm stuffed," Josh finally said, taking a deep breath, "I don't think I could eat another bite."

"Me too."

"You hardly ate anything. Remember how much you ate the last time we came? I couldn't figure out where you put all that food!"

Kelsey laughed, putting down her chopsticks. "Okay, no more stalling. What did you want to tell me?'

"Okay, okay, you're right. I have been stalling. I guess I'm scared about your reaction. It's something I haven't even told your dad, even though I've been wanting to. So, you know how Tina's mom was killed?" He reached across the table and took both of Kelsey's hands in his. Her first instinct was to pull her hands away. Was this a murder confession? Josh looked away, blinking back a tear. He took a deep breath.

"She was my sister."

Wait what? What is he talking about? Okay, Kels, play it cool.

"She was your sister? You mean Anna. Anna was your sister?" Kelsey repeated.

"Our mom, well Anna's mom, got pregnant with me when Anna was in high school. Anna helped our mom deliver me when she was fifteen years old in the living room of the house she grew up in. She took most of her sophomore year of high school off but somehow caught up in summer school to still graduate with her class."

"Anna passed me off as her child because otherwise, I would have been placed into foster care. She pretended she gave birth to me and gave me up for adoption instead. She made sure I went to a good family that was vetted by the top private adoption agency in the area. She gave me my life. I owe her everything."

"But what happened to your mom and dad?"

"Our mom passed away during childbirth, and I don't know who my father is."

"So, Anna's father isn't your father?"

"No, Anna said her father left her mother and that she thinks her mother was seeing someone. That's why I asked for a transfer down here. I wanted to figure out who my father was and to meet Anna. My parents in Seattle had a copy of my original birth certificate and it had Anna's name listed as my mother. It didn't list my father. I contacted Anna when I got to town, and we met twice to talk. I was shocked to find out that she was actually my sister. She didn't know who my father was either. She said that only Leo knew the truth about me being Anna's brother and not her son. I know she trusted him because he was like a big brother to her. When our mom died during childbirth, Leo helped get rid of the body. I don't know if you knew this, but the Eriksen family has ties to an Organized Crime group. I'm not sure how many people know that. Anna told me that Leo's dad did some bad stuff back in the day and Leo was always helping him. I have a feeling someone might be out to hurt Tina and me since we're Anna's only living relatives. That's why I've been careful about who I've told. I mean, I haven't told anyone. I tried telling Tina, but I went about it the wrong way."

"So that's why you kidnapped her? You really scared her, you know? Why didn't you just talk to her while she was in the cabin?"

"Because I didn't know who I could trust. I didn't want both of us to get ambushed in the cabin. I figured we'd go somewhere a little further away to a public place and talk. I wasn't expecting Tina to run from me. I didn't hurt her. At least, I didn't want to. She kicked me in the balls pretty good."

"Wait, back up. Was there a reason that you thought someone was after you and Tina? I understand why Tina was scared. Her mom was murdered and her dad was the main suspect. But did someone threaten you to make you think you were in danger?" Kelsey asked him.

Josh looked down at the table and said, "I got a message."

"What did it say?" Kelsey asked, silently urging Josh to continue. Why was he still holding back?

"I don't know who it was from, but it was a text that told me to go back to Seattle."

Kelsey stopped to think for a minute. *This all made sense. Tina and Josh were stated in the will as her main beneficiaries. If Tina and Josh were no longer around, who would get Anna's estate? Wouldn't it just go to probate?*

"Did you tell my dad?" Kelsey asked.

"Yeah, I did. When I was trying to explain to him why I took Tina. I don't think he heard me, though. He didn't care about my excuse. He was pretty mad at me, Kelsey." Josh said, shaking his head. He knew he screwed up.

"We're going to get to the bottom of this, I promise—for you and for Tina."

This time, it was Kelsey's turn to hold Josh's hands and reassure him. "I'm on your team, you know. You don't have to keep things from me, even if I am the chief's daughter."

They walked back to Josh's car. The air was balmy—it was perfect fall weather, even if it was a little humid. Kelsey took a deep breath and got into the Camaro.

"How about an after-dinner drink at my place?" Josh asked, hoping she would say yes. Ever since he was suspended from the department, he had felt more alone than ever. Being with Kelsey gave him hope for the future. She was everything he had ever wanted in a girlfriend.

"Sure. I'd love that," Kelsey replied.

Chapter 67

Wednesday, October 5, 2022

Kelsey's stomach did little butterflies as they reached Josh's apartment complex. Their relationship had moved relatively quickly in the past weeks but this was the first time she would be going to his place. Josh led her into the main lobby where they took two flights of stairs up to the third floor. The smells of apartment living reminded Kelsey of her college days. From roasted chicken to Italian parmesan, every door they passed emitted different smells. Josh's apartment was at the end of the hall. He opened the door guiding Kelsey in before him. As they entered, Kelsey noticed the apartment was cozy and smelled of Josh's woodsy cologne. She sat on the brown leather couch as Josh selected a bottle of wine and two glasses. The fruit-forward cabernet was a pleasant surprise on Kelsey's tongue as she savored the first sip. She swirled her glass around and around, staring at the thick legs gliding down the curve of the glass.

"What's on your mind? I can tell you're thinking about something," Josh said, watching as Kelsey savored another small sip.

Kelsey put her wine glass down on the table.

"I want to ask you a question and if you say no, it's fine."

"Ohhh-kay."

"I think we should do a DNA test to determine who your father is," Kelsey said.

"Whose DNA would we compare it to?" Josh asked. "Even if you have my DNA, they would need other DNA to compare it to, right?"

"Well, there *is* a whole police DNA database. Plus, it may be someone close to the family. Leo's wife, Mae thinks Leo was your biological father."

"Whoa! But she had no idea it was Anna's mom's baby—not Anna's. Who do we think my father could be? Not Leo, right? He would be a little young for my mother."

"We can't one hundred percent rule Leo out, but my guess is that it's unlikely he's your father."

"Makes sense. Should I ask your dad what the next step is?"

"No need. I've got the test right here," Kelsey said, grinning, as she removed a swab kit from her bag.

Chapter 68

K elsey unclasped Fin's leash and walked toward the kitchen to help Tina with the lasagna. The house smelled like an Italian restaurant. Tina could barely hold it in and started asking Kelsey questions a mile a minute about her dinner with Josh. As Kelsey washed and dried her hands, she recapped the conversation.

"Josh is my uncle?" Tina said.

"That's what Josh told me. That's what your mom told him."

Tina sat on a bar stool and tapped her finger to her chin. "So, my grandmother got pregnant by some guy. Who are we comparing Josh's DNA to?"

"My dad said they would compare it to all the DNA samples from the case. And they already had Leo's on file. Apparently, he has an extensive arrest record. The only one they don't have is Mae's. They'll also test his DNA against the Scotts' DNA. They have your dad and Abby's DNA on file."

Tina rolled her eyes. "Don't even get me started with Leo and his record. He's made so many stupid decisions in life, it's unbelievable. Maybe we should ask my Aunt Mae if she found anything out."

"That's a good idea," Kelsey said. "And we should probably keep it a secret for now that your mom is not Josh's mother."

"I'll call Mae once we put all the food in the oven," Tina said, nodding.

"Do you think we should ask Leo about it, too? Since he was okay with me interviewing him, maybe we could ask him if we could talk to him off the record," Kelsey said.

"But what if he's the killer?"

"Why would he kill your mom? Right now, there's no motive for anyone except you or Josh. You both stand to inherit your mom's estate."

"True. But why would either of us kill her for the house and the money she had in the bank? I know the killer is not me, and I don't think it's Josh, either. He just met my mom. He would have no idea of her net worth even if she was rich. And he probably didn't know he was even in her will. Ugh, I feel like we're going in circles," Tina said as she slid the lasagna into the preheated oven and Kelsey basted the halved French loaf with melted garlic butter and parsley.

"Okay, here goes," Tina said, licking some marinara off her thumb and setting her phone on the countertop.

"Hello? Tina, is that you?" Mae answered as Tina clicked the speaker on her phone so Kelsey could listen in.

"Hi, Auntie Mae. Yes, it's me. Have I caught you at a bad time?"

"Oh no, I'm just getting my nails done. They were a wreck, and I've been so busy that this is the only time I could do them.

Are you okay, honey? Do you need anything? I know Leo and I haven't been around lately, but you let us know if you need something, okay?"

"Okay, thank you, Auntie. I have a question for you. Did you find out any more about the baby that my mom had?" Tina asked.

"I did some digging, and it turns out he's a police officer right here in Oakview. Josh deLuca. Can you believe it?"

Tina looked at Kelsey, who nodded and pointed to herself, mouthing, "Tell her about Josh and me."

"About that. I received the copy of my mom's will you mailed me. It's such a small world. It turns out that Kelsey is dating Josh. She had no idea he was part of our family."

"Well, he's not. Not really. Your mother gave him away."

Tina's face flushed red, and Kelsey motioned for her to take a deep breath.

"If I tell you something, Tina, you must promise not to tell anyone. Especially your father. Understand?"

"Of course. I promise."

"Your Uncle Leo had been sending money to Anna for several years. A few months ago, he accidentally left his laptop open, and I saw the money transfers each month. He has to be the child's father."

Kelsey's jaw dropped, and Tina thought about what she would say next. *Why would her uncle be sending her mom money?*

"Are you sure?"

"Yes, dear. One hundred percent. I told him to knock it off. She doesn't need his money. Her company has grown, and she has plenty of it. Leo is not made of money. I don't know why he would give her money other than to keep her mouth shut about the boy."

"You think my mother was blackmailing Uncle Leo?" Tina said, shocked.

"Oh, honey, it makes perfect sense. I love you, but you have got to stop being so naïve about these types of things."

"But do you really think ..."

"Tina, I've got to go. Think about what I said, though, okay? Text me if you have any other questions. I want to find out who killed your mother just as much as you do."

"Okay, Auntie. Bye."

Tina turned to Kelsey and said, "This is getting even weirder. Why would Uncle Leo send my mom money each month? We know the baby is not Mom's. Do you think Leo *is* the father? Eww, that's kind of gross. My grandmother and Leo?"

"Can you get into your mom's bank account so we can take a look at the payments?" Kelsey asked.

"Yes, I have her log-in," Tina said, walking over to her laptop.

Tina logged into her mom's account, and she and Kelsey scoured it for deposits and transfers. After over an hour of looking, Tina said, "There's nothing there. Where would Leo be sending money to?"

"What about her business account?" Kelsey asked.

"It's worth trying. The problem is, I don't have access to that. I can get the account number, but I don't know the log-in details. I don't know why Leo would send it to my mom's work account."

"I have an idea," Kelsey said, sending a quick text.

When you get a chance, can you call me?

Her phone rang a few seconds later.

"Hey, Sam, thanks for calling. I have a question for you. How hard is it to hack into someone's business bank account? For information, not to make a transaction."

"Well, it's illegal. But aside from that, it's not that hard. It depends on the bank," Sam said.

"Hmm, okay."

"I'll see you for our training session tomorrow. We'll talk then."

Chapter 69

Friday, October 7, 2022

"Sorry, I didn't want to discuss breaking into bank accounts over the phone," Sam said as he foam-rolled on the floor. "Our devices listen to everything we say."

"I get it. I don't want to get you in trouble, so if you wanted to write down how to do it, I could try and do it myself," Kelsey said.

After she explained why she was asking him about hacking into a bank account, Sam considered it. "You just want to look? Not transfer or deposit?" Kelsey nodded.

"I can do that. I have everything set up at my place to do it. Do you and Tina want to come over at lunch today? Does one o'clock work?" Sam said in a low voice.

"Sam, are you sure?" Kelsey whispered.

"Yeah, it's not that hard. You just have to know what you're doing."

Chapter 70

K elsey rang the doorbell to Sam's Oakview Hills mansion. She and Tina took in the majestic building with white pillars and a beautiful cherub fountain in its long driveway. Sam answered the door and showed them in. Climbing up a huge flight of stairs, Sam guided them into a bedroom full of computer equipment.

"Where do you even sleep?" Kelsey asked him.

"Oh, this is my computer room. There are three other bedrooms," Sam laughed. "Don't you know any other tech nerds?"

"Not to this extent. This room is insane. In a good way." There were three screens on his desk and another three on the wall. The gentle whir of fans could be heard as they kept the hard drives cool.

After Sam swore them both to secrecy, Tina showed Sam a screenshot of a check her mom had written her a few months ago. The account was from Anna's business account, AJT Holdings. Using the bank and account information, Sam typed a few things into his computer and then turned around to ask

Tina, "You don't know your mom's password, do you? Because that would make it a lot easier. I can bypass the two-factor authentication easily, but the password is the hardest part."

"My mom's password for almost everything is 'MyGirlTina1999'. But I don't know because this is her business account, not her personal," Tina said.

Sam clicked a few buttons and said, "Nope. Not it. All of the words start with caps, right?

"Usually. But maybe try it with all lower case or upper case?" Tina said.

Sam tried a few more times, trying not to get locked out. Finally, he said, "It's alternating upper and lower case letters. Now, just to get rid of the two-factor authentication. And we're in. Let's try to get this done as quickly as possible."

Tina sat down and started scrolling through her mom's statements. Everything looked normal, and she could see the money transfers from Leo each month for a few thousand dollars. The money was transferred out to another account as quickly as it went in. The name on the account was Joshua DeLuca, Living Trust.

"The money *was* sent to an account for Josh," Tina said.

"Leo sent money to Anna to send to Josh. If he is, in fact, Josh's father, this would make sense. Although Mae thought the baby's mother was Anna," said Kelsey, thinking out loud.

"Look here. Back in 2018, there was a big deposit of twenty-five thousand. It was from Leo's company, Eriksen Contractors. It doesn't look like it was sent to Josh's account," Tina said. "What could that have been for?"

Chapter 71

O n the way back to Saffron's house, Kelsey and Tina stopped at Anna's house for Tina to pick up a few more personal items. As they entered, Kelsey noticed everything had been cleaned up from the last time she was there. There weren't any more police markers, and the police tape outside had been removed. Tina headed straight for the closet in Anna's room. She pushed the clothes to one side. A few pieces of kindergarten artwork were pinned to the closet's back wall. As Tina carefully removed the artwork, a small safe appeared. Tina dialed the combination, and after two tries, the safe opened. She reached in and removed a thick mailing envelope.

"My mom kept all of her important documents in here: my birth certificate, her birth certificate, and our passports. This envelope is thick, so I'm sure there are some other important things in here," Tina said as she peered into the envelope.

She crouched down next to the bed, pulled the throw rug up, and then stood and stomped on the floor. A loose floorboard popped up, and Tina pulled it out. Kelsey gasped.

"What's wrong?" Tina said, surprised.

"Remember that night Justin and I came here and found Jason's phone, and your aunt was here?"

"Yeah. She was looking for his phone, right?"

"Sure. That's what she told everyone. But she knew about this hiding spot. Justin and I could hear her stomp on the floor just like you did, and then she grunted while pulling the board up. I think she was here for something other than Jason's phone."

"My aunt knows about this hiding spot?" Tina said as the color drained from her face.

Tina knelt on the ground, stuck her arm in the hole, and reached inside.

At first glance, anyone who stumbled upon the removable floorboard would think it was just a hole in the floor, but the hole swallowed Tina's arm whole before she finally started pulling it out.

She let out a big sigh of relief and said, "Okay. It's still here. That's good."

Pulling out a large lockbox, Tina opened it, peeked inside, and nodded. Standing up, she said, "My mom had a lot of secret hiding places. It looks like we're going to have some fun tonight."

Tina walked into her bedroom, and Kelsey followed. "I should probably take a couple of work outfits, too, since I might have to go into the office a couple of times a week—at least to pick up and drop off work."

"Of course. Take your time," Kelsey said.

Tina took a duffel bag out of her closet and began stuffing various pieces of clothing into it.

"Do you need help with anything?" Kelsey asked.

"I'm a little freaked out about the downstairs since that's where my mom died. I mean, I know the cleaners were here and did a very thorough job, but still. Do you think you could go down there and check things out?" Tina asked.

As Kelsey walked through the downstairs, she paid close attention to anything that seemed out of place. She flipped through a few coffee table books and looked under the couch and loveseat with her phone's flashlight. The living room was simple and modern, with no picture frames or trinkets. Kelsey moved on to the kitchen which was still in pristine condition. A laptop sat on the kitchen counter near the refrigerator, its charging cord placed neatly on top. Kelsey continued to poke around, looking in all the drawers and cabinets, the refrigerator and freezer, the dishwasher, and the microwave. Everything was empty, except a few cleaning products and sponges which remained under the kitchen sink.

Kelsey grabbed the laptop and charger and headed back up to Tina's room.

"Is that my mom's laptop? The police must have returned it. It's probably stripped of everything," Tina said.

"I don't think that's how it works. I think they just snoop and look for suspicious things or clues. They don't wipe the whole computer."

"Really? I thought they took all the information," Tina said, shrugging.

"So, you know that fridge you guys have?" Kelsey asked.

Tina burst out laughing. "You mean the Monstrous 3000? Kels, you have no idea. My mom was obsessed with getting one of those. It's like majorly expensive. I think she was in love with it."

She continued, "My mom saved up for months for that thing. She got it for less than they normally go for. My Uncle Leo hooked her up because he works with a lot of big-name vendors. I don't know why she liked it so much."

"Hey, so you know how your mom liked to hide stuff?"

Tina looked at Kelsey wide-eyed and shrugged, "Well, it wouldn't hurt to check."

They got to work opening drawers and removing shelves but found nothing unusual. They even tugged at the drip pan. Kelsey searched online for directions on removing it, but the drip pan wasn't removable on this type of refrigerator. As Tina slid a glass shelf back in, her knee knocked the control panel for the produce drawer. The panel popped up at the edge, and they looked at each other wide-eyed. Carefully, they removed the control panel to reveal a small gold key.

Chapter 72

Kelsey and Tina ran straight to Tina's room at Saffron's house and wasted no time in getting to work. Tina opened the lockbox and inside was a neatly stacked wad of cash. "It's fifty thousand," Tina explained, "Her emergency fund."

The box also contained two flash drives and a solid-state hard drive. Tina handed them to Kelsey who inserted the first flash drive into Tina's laptop. Both flash drives contained extensive photo collections documenting memories from 2000 to the present.

Next, they turned their attention to the solid-state drive which served as a backup storage device for Anna's business. Kelsey and Tina sifted through the files, but they were a mundane collection of bookkeeping spreadsheets and copies of invoices. The sheer volume of data was overwhelming, yet it offered little in the way of immediate clues. They shared a look of frustration, knowing they needed to dig deeper to find anything that might help.

Suddenly, the Windows jingle played, and Kelsey and Tina looked at Anna's computer as it started to boot up. It was an old computer and took a few minutes to start. The password screen appeared, and Tina typed it in. The laptop's wallpaper showed Anna and Tina at the beach. The picture looked pretty recent. Tina sat, staring at the screen.

"Are you okay?" Kelsey asked, rubbing Tina's back.

"Yeah, sorry. I just remember when this picture was taken. It was this summer. Only a few months ago. My mom was still alive then." Tina let out a big breath.

A folder on the desktop was labeled 'AJT Holdings'. Tina opened the folder to reveal dated files named 'Invoice', followed by different company names. Tina clicked on the first one. The invoice was dated August 10, 2022—about a month before Anna's death. According to the itemization, it was for thirty hours of billed consulting for a project called Anime Time and was marked paid on September 9, 2022.

"Does your mom have a website?" Kelsey asked.

Tina searched "AJT Holdings." The top listing was AJT Consulting. Tina clicked the link. A professional website loaded with stock photos of people at desks and computers and a description of the company's services. Anna's headshot and bio appeared when Tina clicked on the About Us page. Her title was listed as CEO and founder. Under that, Leo Eriksen and Nick Scott were listed as the CFO and CMO, respectively.

Tina stared at the web page. Her dad. And her Uncle Leo. They were part of her mom's business.

"Uh, oh," Kelsey said.

241

"I think I need to call my dad," Tina said, reaching for her phone, but Kelsey stopped her.

"What if ...?" Kelsey asked.

"There is no way my dad killed my mom or is in on it. My uncles and aunts? Sure, maybe. I would even put Jason on that list before I put my dad on it. No one understood how much he actually loved my mom."

Kelsey nodded, and Tina dialed her dad's number.

"Tina!" he answered, "Hi, baby. I'm so happy to hear from you."

"Hey, Dad," she said. "I'm so sorry I haven't called earlier. This whole thing with Mom has me rattled. I want to tell you everything, but it'll have to wait for a later time. I have some questions to ask you if that's okay."

"Of course. But first, how are you doing? Where are you staying? Can we meet for lunch or something? You know I was cleared of your mom's death, right?"

"I'm okay. I'm staying with friends, but I'm kind of hiding out since the killer hasn't been found yet. I'm glad you were cleared of Mom's death. I kept telling the police it wasn't you."

"I love you, Tina. Always know that. I don't care if I'm not your biological father. You're still my little girl and you always will be," Nick said, sounding choked up and emotional. He took a deep breath and continued, "So, what do you want to ask me?"

"So, you know Mom had a consulting company, right?"

"Yes, she started that as a side gig, but it took off—big time. She told you about it, right?"

"She did, but I guess I never really paid attention to what her job even was. Her website looks legit."

"Oh. That. I helped her design it. We thought having a professional website would really put her on the map. I was so proud of her when her business started taking off."

"Wow, really? She didn't talk about it unless she signed a big contract. I just stumbled upon the company website now on her laptop. It says you're CMO, and Uncle Leo is CFO. Why didn't you or Mom tell me about this?"

"Honestly, I forgot about that until you just brought it up. Your mom thought it would make the company look more robust if she had other people on the site. Your Uncle Leo agreed to help her with the financial side of it. He gave her money to start the company, and I designed her website, so she made me CMO. I didn't do too much marketing for her after that. An ad here or there to put on social media or Google, but she pretty much ran the whole thing herself. I don't think Leo did any of her bookkeeping, come to think of it. Your mom did everything on her own."

"So, it was a real company? And you owned it with Mom and Leo?"

"Yes, it's a real company. And Leo and I are silent partners. Anna knew she could trust both of us. And Tina, she made a lot of money. I was so proud of her. Your mom finally found her niche."

"Why was Uncle Leo giving her money monthly for the past several years?"

"The past several years? No, he just loaned her money to start the business. I don't even remember how much it was. It was back when she started it in 2018. Maybe a few thousand for startup costs. I'm sure she's already paid him back by now. Your mom didn't need money, Tina. In fact, I'm embarrassed even to tell you this. She gave me money to help with some gambling debt I had. I still have more to pay off, but the money she gave me helped buy me some time. Your mom was a good person."

"She lent you money, or she gave it to you?"

"She gave it to me. She was giving me money in installments so it wouldn't raise a red flag when it came to her doing her taxes. She didn't want it to look like she was withdrawing large sums from her account. Tina, why are you asking me all of this?"

"Do you think her murder had something to do with the company? It sounds like you and Uncle Leo would benefit if Mom died."

"Tina Marie Scott! I can't believe you would think either one of us would kill your mom for her company. Your mom is the only one who knows how to run it. The company will need to be dissolved. I have no idea how much it's worth, and I'm sure Leo doesn't either. We both loved your mom."

"I'm sorry, Dad. I know you didn't do it. Deep down, I don't think Uncle Leo did it either. I just don't know any other motive than money. Or maybe some kind of revenge?"

"Revenge? On your mom? I don't even know where to start with that."

"That's why I was going with the money angle. I can't imagine Mom doing anything wrong," Tina said. "I love you, Dad. And I miss you. I just want to find out who killed Mom. We'll have lunch soon, okay? I promise."

"I miss you too, honey. I'll call Leo and see what he says about the company. Maybe he was doing her books, after all," Nick replied.

"Do you know if Mom had a safety deposit box?" Tina asked on the off chance that was what the little gold key went to.

"You found the key," Nick said, his voice low.

"What is it for?" Tina asked.

"Your mom hid the key and wouldn't tell anyone where it was including me. It's for a safety deposit box at the Bank of America in Downtown Oakview. Box 5724."

"Do you know what's in it?"

"No, but whatever it is, it's for you, honey. She knew if someone was going to find the key, it would be you."

Tina and Kelsey looked at each other in shock after they hung up. They looked at the clock. 6:02. It was too late to go to the bank today. Instead, they turned their attention to the envelope. The contents slid out onto the floor to reveal birth certificates, passports, insurance documents, and business documents. One of the birth certificates belonged to Josh, and Kelsey picked it up.

"I wish we had known about these before doing all the dirty work," Kelsey said. "All this time, your mom had a copy of his birth certificate. His original one. And look! The adoption papers. Josh was adopted by the DeLucas only two and a half months after he was born. Both the DeLucas and your mom signed the documents in December of 1990. Who took care of him during that time? It must have been your mom and maybe even Leo."

"I wish we knew if the whole Josh thing was related to my mom's death."

"I think the fact that he received that awful message means it's clear that whoever did this knows about Josh, and he might even be next." Kelsey felt a knot in her stomach form as she realized what she just said. She picked up her phone to text him.

hey, be safe, ok? I don't want anything happening to u. xo

whoa! where did that come from? are u ok?

yeah, i just remembered the awful threatening message you got

im not really worried about myself. im more worried about Tina. she's tough, but i carry a gun and am trained to be more aware than the average person. don't know if u noticed, but i always choose a table with my back to the wall

Kelsey thought about this for a minute.

wow. ur right. didn't notice that until you mentioned in now. ur amazing

ur more amazing. Dinner tomorrow night? promised Chelsea id watch a movie with her tonight u in Seattle?

Lol. No, we sit on Facetime and watch the same movie at the same time together

That is so sweet!

I miss her a lot.

I bet. ok, going to get back to doing detective work with Tina. talk to u later.

xo

XOXO

Chapter 73

Friday, October 7, 2022

"Whoa, look at this," Tina said, and Kelsey scooted closer to see. It was a photocopy of a letter Anna wrote to Josh.

"I wonder if she ever got a chance to give the original to him when they met," Kelsey said.

October 21, 2000

Dear Josh,

My name is Anna, and I'm your big sister. Our mom died after she gave birth to you, and so I took care of you for the first few months of your life. You were a really happy baby and I loved you so much. My friend Leo helped to take care of you, too. He's like a big brother to me, so I guess that means he's kind of a big brother to you, too. I was only fifteen years old when you were born, so I knew that I would have to give you up for adoption. I didn't want you going to a foster home, so that's why I pretended like I was your mom and not your sister. Leo has connections so we were able to use a very private, very exclusive adoption agency to get you into a good home. I hope I get to see you again one day, but in case I don't, I wanted to write this letter so you would know more about our family.

Our mom's name was Angela Kiel. And my dad's name was Joseph Kiel. I don't think my dad is your dad though because he left me and our mom the year before you were even conceived.

I think Mom was seeing someone but I don't know who and I think that's who your dad was. Mom didn't go out very much so I think it's someone she already knew. I hope one day you can find out who your father is.

You have a niece. My daughter Tina was born last year to me and my husband Nick Scott.

If you get this letter, please try to find her.

Our "big brother" Leo is married to Mae Scott, my husband Nick's twin sister. Abby Scott is their other sister, and she is married to David Crenshaw. They have a toddler named Jason. Franklin is the fourth sibling in the Scott crew. He moved to North Carolina to serve in the military when he was eighteen years old. He doesn't keep in contact with any of us. I'm going to attach all of the contact information I have for everyone in hopes that you'll get this letter one day. I have never stopped thinking of you and I hope you are doing well with your new family, the DeLucas.

I love you, little brother,

Anna

Chapter 74

Saturday, October 8, 2022

Nine a.m. Josh's phone rang. He looked at the caller ID. *Randy James.* Taking a deep breath, he answered.

"Hello, sir."

"Josh, it's Chief James. Would you mind coming down to the station?"

"Uh, now? Right now?" Josh said. He felt like his knees were going to buckle. Was he getting fired?

"If you can. We got the DNA results in."

Josh took a sigh of relief and replied, "Yes, sir. I'll be there in under ten minutes."

"Great. See you then."

***

Josh arrived at the station, and Miriam buzzed him in.

"Come in, Josh. Have a seat," Randy said as he sat behind his desk. He opened a manila envelope.

"You got the results back that quickly?"

"Well, I may have called in a favor. I disapprove of what happened with you and Tina, but I genuinely think you're a good guy, Josh. I know you make Kelsey happy, and she's a pretty good judge of character. I want to help you find your family. I also want to find out who killed your sister."

"I appreciate it, sir," Josh said.

"Okay then. Let's get on with this. The DNA results show that you are related to the Eriksens. Sven Eriksen is your father. Leo is your brother."

Josh and Randy sat in silence, staring at each other. Josh swallowed.

"This is a lot to take in," Josh said, and Randy nodded. "Thank you, sir. I appreciate it.

Can I tell Kelsey?"

"Of course. That information is yours to tell who you wish. I want to warn you that Sven is not in the best mental state. We interviewed him and he became angry with Hart. Just tread lightly if you decide you're going to see him."

"I understand, sir." Josh stood to shake Randy's hand.

"On another note, Josh, I'd like you to return to work. After fully investigating the situation, the agency has decided that your actions will not be held against you. You'll find next week's schedule in the app."

"Thank you so much, sir. I won't let you down, and nothing like this will ever happen again," Josh said.

"I know it won't. You come to me from now on if you need help with something like that. You hear me?"

"Yessir. I do."

Chapter 75

Saturday, October 8, 2022

"What the hell?" Kelsey said, sitting on one of the gym benches.

Josh put his head in his hands and said, "I know. Crazy, right?"

"So crazy!" Kelsey said, walking away to a training session. "We're so close but still so far away. And we still don't know what any of this has to do with Anna's death."

Things were so much simpler back in Seattle. But Josh wouldn't give Kelsey up for the world. He was deep in thought when Kelsey ran back over to him. He jumped, and Kelsey giggled.

"I thought you were in a session," he said.

"I am. Sammy had to use the restroom, and I just thought of something. We should have a big family dinner so you and Tina can meet without your fake mustache."

Josh's face turned serious. He said, "I think that is the best idea I've heard this year, Kelsey. Let's do it."

Kelsey's phone pinged and up popped a message from Tina.

went to the bank and opened the safety deposit box. when's ur next break?

Chapter 76

Saturday, October 8, 2022

After picking Finley up from her condo, Kelsey drove over to Saffron's house. She knocked, and Tina let her in. There was an air of excitement as Tina pulled Kelsey into the bedroom. Spread across Tina's bed was what looked like a million dollars. There were piles of one-hundred-dollar bills in neat piles. Kelsey's eyes widened, and she looked at Tina who had a big grin. Alongside the cash were two pieces of paper. Tina carefully picked one up and handed it to Kelsey.

October 10, 2000

Dear Tina,

I know your dad always tells you I'm crazy about hiding money. If you're reading this it means:

- *I'm no longer living, or*

- *You found the key to the box, or*

- *Your dad told you what the key went to*

I originally started this collection of money as your wedding fund. I began by putting five dollars a week into the box and then more as my company grew. But after careful thought, I realized that this money could be used for whatever your heart desired. You don't have to get married to enjoy it. Please know that being your mother has been the best thing in my life. I love you so much. I hope you never have to read this letter, and that we can enjoy the money together someday, but in case that doesn't happen, please always live life to the fullest and never look back.

Love, Mom

Kelsey's eyes teared up, and she looked up at Tina, who had tears streaming down her face. Tina took the letter from Kelsey and handed her the second letter.

September 5, 2022

Dear Tina,

If you're reading this, it means I'm gone. I didn't tell you who your biological father was after taking the tests because I didn't want any more lives to be affected by my actions. I regret telling your dad, Nick, but I didn't think it was fair for him not to know. Only your biological father knows that you are his. It's Randy James. Yes, Kelsey's dad. I know Kelsey is the sister you've always wanted, and it warms my heart that you have found each other and have such a strong bond.

Love you always,

Mama

Tina and Kelsey sat down to count the money on the bed. The total came to just under a million dollars.

Chapter 77

Sunday, October 9, 2022

It was farmers market day, and Kelsey was heading out with Fin and Justin. Along the way, they ran into Kelsey's neighbor, Brooke, and her miniature dachshund, Mickey. They let Fin and Mickey play and watched as Finley tried to tame the wild little dog.

Kelsey laughed, "They're so cute together."

"They are. It's hilarious," Brooke said. "Hey, I was thinking about joining the gym. This peri-menopausal belly is no joke."

Kelsey gave Brooke some pointers on how to deal with the changes her body was going through. The biggest one was getting enough protein during meals.

"Thanks, Kelsey! I'll pay more attention to that. I'll pop by Fox this week when I get a chance," Brooke said.

After saying their goodbyes, Justin said, "Another new client, huh? You're on a roll."

"Yeah, and remember Audrey, my client Caroline's daughter? She's starting to train with me this week, too," Kelsey said.

"Oh, yeah, I remember her," Justin said, but how he didn't look at Kelsey told her he was hiding something.

"Justin! What are you not telling me?" Kelsey said, looking at him straight in the eyes as his face turned beet red. "No! Are you two dating?"

"Shh. Don't say it that loud."

"Why? There's no one around. You're being silly. Aww, Jus! I'm happy for you. So, how many dates has it been? Did you kiss her?"

"It's only been one date. Stop making such a big deal of it. Audrey's a nice person. We had a good time. That's all you're getting out of me, Kelsey Sue."

"Justin's got a girlfriend. Justin's got a girlfriend," Kelsey sang teasingly. She bounded up the steps with Finley and grabbed her fanny pack.

***

"What are you getting today?" Kelsey asked as they walked down the aisle.

"Probably some OJ to bring to your parents' house and some veggies for meal prep this week. That's it."

Kelsey turned to pick out a few zucchinis from her favorite stand. One thing she knew how to make well was her taco-stuffed zucchinis. Even Justin said they were delicious. As she reached for a zucchini, another hand reached for the same one.

"Oops, sorry," Kelsey said as she pulled her hand back. She looked at the other woman and realized it was Aunt Mae. *Well, this is awkward.*

"Well, if it isn't Tina's personal trainer. Hello again, Kelsey," Mae said, her arms wrapped around bundles of kale and lettuce and her hands carrying bags of various other vegetables.

"Hi, Mae." Kelsey turned to see Leo standing behind Mae, looking bored out of his mind. "Hi, Leo. How are you both this morning?"

"Oh, we're fine. Just fine. Aren't we dear?" Mae said, shoving the produce into Leo's arms. Kelsey glanced up at Leo who shrugged.

"Well, we're off. I'm making a vegetable soup for dinner tonight. One hundred percent vegan," Mae said, looking proud of herself. Leo made a finger down his throat gesture to Kelsey behind Mae's back.

Kelsey chuckled at Leo's expression and said, "Okay, then, have a delicious dinner."

Once Mae and Leo walked away with their zucchini, Justin said, "Well, that was awkward."

"No kidding. She's such a weirdo. He's funny, though. I have a feeling she tells him what to do, and he does it. I bet his sending Anna money was a huge sore spot in their relationship."

Chapter 78

Sunday, October 9, 2022

"Hi, Dad," said Kelsey as she hugged him and took her coat off. The scent of freshly made waffles and crispy bacon filled the air. Kelsey's stomach growled.

"Hi, honey. Hi, Justin. And how's my favorite grandpup? Your mom and Brian are in the kitchen. Here, let me take that OJ from you, Justin. Ooh, fresh squeezed. I'm going to like this."

"Best OJ in town," Justin said as he followed Randy and Kelsey into the kitchen.

"So, Justin has a new girlfriend," Kelsey blurted out. Justin's face immediately turned red as he glared at Kelsey.

"It was one date. Stop it," Justin said. "Speaking of girl-friends, you got anyone on the radar, Bri?"

"Stop changing the subject," Kelsey said.

"I kind of like this girl in a couple of my classes. Her name is Sayra. Mom took me and her for ice cream on Friday because our football team had a bye."

"See? Brian's proud of having a girlfriend. Why aren't you?" Kelsey said, loving that she was pushing Justin's buttons.

Justin grunted, then said, "That's awesome, Brian. Is she smart?"

Brian nodded and added, "And pretty." Justin gave him a fist bump.

"Okay, everyone, brunch is ready. We have pancakes, waffles, eggs, bacon, and all the toppings," Joanna said as she placed the platter of scrambled eggs on the table.

"Hey, Dad. I was thinking we should have a dinner so that everyone can meet Tina," Kelsey said.

"That's a great idea, Kelsey. Joanna, what do you think?" Randy asked his wife.

"That sounds like a wonderful idea. I'd love to meet her." Joanna replied. "What did you have in mind, Kelsey?"

"What about dinner tonight at Frontier Tavern? Six? I can double-check with Josh and Tina," Kelsey said, taking her phone out to text them both.

"No phones at the table, missy!" Joanna said, shooing away Kelsey's phone.

"Sorry, Mom," Kelsey said, putting her phone down.

After brunch, Brian and Justin helped Joanna clean up, and Randy summoned Kelsey into his home office.

"What's up, Dad? Everything okay?" Kelsey asked.

"There's one thing that's been bothering me. Why was Leo paying Anna for Josh if Sven was the kid's father? And who stands to benefit from Anna's death? Right now, it's Tina and Josh."

"But Leo and Nick are owners of Anna's company, Dad. Tina and I just found out and she called her dad to confirm. Nick has gambling debt, and Leo is just Leo. I haven't come up with a motive for him yet but obviously he has a shady past," Kelsey said. "It's killing me that we don't know the missing piece of the puzzle."

"You and me both, kid," Randy said.

Chapter 79

Sunday, October 9, 2022

Leo unlocked the front door, holding the bags of fresh vegetables from the farmers' market. Mae stormed in behind him. The phone call she took in the car put her in a bad mood. How could Leo not be the child's father? She was sure the test was wrong. When Tina told her that Sven was the father, Mae nearly lost it.

"It's a coincidence we ran into Tina's trainer, isn't it?" Leo said. "I like her. It's good that Tina has someone like that in her life, don't you think?"

Mae was off in her own little world, staring at an invisible spot on the butcher block.

"Mae!" Leo said, and her head popped up. "Did you just hear what I said? What's wrong?"

"Why were you sending Anna money if the baby wasn't yours? He's not your responsibility."

Leo took Mae's hands and guided her over to the kitchen table.

"Honey, what are you talking about? Where is this coming from?"

"Leo! Tina told me the child isn't even Anna's. It's her mother's. I also know you've been sending Anna money all these years. I saw the transfers in your bank account. She didn't need your money. She made plenty of money building the company you helped her start. You never saw a penny of that. But *you're* sending *her* money? I don't believe it was for the kid. There, I've said it. You're hiding something and I won't be a part of it. I work too hard for my husband to be giving money to another woman," Mae said, violently wiping away the tears.

"Mae, let me explain. It's not what you think," Leo said, but Mae put her hand out, stood up, and went into the bedroom, slamming the door.

Chapter 80

Sunday, October 9, 2022

Kelsey pulled on the new gray sweater dress that had been sitting in her closet for two seasons. The weather outside was blustery so this was the perfect evening to wear it paired with some knee-high black boots.

"Wow!" Tina said to Kelsey as she climbed into Chuckie. "You look nice in a dress. I don't think I've ever seen you in one."

"I don't wear them often. Mostly to special occasions. But I do have a few."

"I like the belt. Very chic," Tina observed.

"Well, thank you. I try! Usually, Saffron helps me with my outfits. She's so much better at fashion than I am."

"Who do you think helped me put this together?" Tina said, opening her arms to reveal a cute new blouse with the perfect necklace, jeans, and boots to match.

"Not surprised."

"I'm so glad we're sisters."

"Me too. I couldn't ask for anyone better. I'm excited for you to meet everyone. Just be yourself. I can tell you're nervous. I do the same thing," Kelsey said as she pointed to Tina's tapping foot. She reached over and squeezed Tina's hand.

As they entered the restaurant, Kelsey spotted her family at a table. Randy was waving his arms wildly at her. *What a goofball. That must be where I get it from.*

"Hi, guys. This is Tina. Tina, this is, well, you know, my dad. Our dad. This is my mom, Joanna, and our brother Brian."

"It's very nice to meet you, Tina. I've heard wonderful things about you," Joanna said, smiling.

"Thank you, Joanna. I've heard nice things about all of you, too."

Brian smiled at Tina and said, "Hey."

Tina gave him a "hey" right back.

Randy stood up as Josh approached the table. He shook Randy's hand. He had three small bouquets and handed one each to Joanna, Kelsey, and Tina.

"You are such a gifter," Kelsey said.

"Guilty as charged," Josh said as he made eye contact with Tina.

"Hi, I don't think we've formally met. I'm Josh."

"Hi. Tina," she said.

Josh sat down, and an awkward silence hovered over the table as everyone reviewed their menus.

"Okay, I'm going to break the ice since the energy in here is making me uncomfortable. We all know what happened and how everyone is related to who. And we've all hung out together with the exception of Tina. I know Josh feels bad about how he tried to talk to Tina, and she thought he was attacking her, so let's just get that out on the table."

Josh gave a sigh of relief. "Thank you, Kelsey. Yeah, I do feel extremely bad about what happened, Tina. I would never, ever hurt you. I was so scared someone was coming after both of us. First, your mom was killed, and then I got a message to leave town. It scared the crap out of me. It wasn't right. And it wasn't professional. I'm sorry."

"I'm sorry, too. For kicking you in the balls," Tina replied.

Brian, unable to hold it in, burst out laughing. "OMG," he said, "she kicked you in the balls, dude? That probably fuckin' hurt!"

"Language, young man!" Joanna interjected.

"Sorry, Mom," Brian said, but he was still chuckling.

Josh chuckled and mouthed to Brian, "Hurt like a mother-fucker," which made Brian crack up even more.

"Okay, okay you two. Sorry, Tina. Continue," Joanna said.

"I hope we can become friends because you're my only family on my mom's side that I know of."

"I'd like that too," Josh said, giving Tina a sincere smile.

"Great job, Kels," Randy said. "You always were the one to hate uncomfortable silences. Thank goodness you have a big mouth."

"Randy!" Joanna scolded.

"Josh, what's this about a note to leave town?" Randy said with one inquisitive eyebrow up. "You never told me this."

"I know. At first, I thought it was a joke. And then I realized that someone had probably connected me to Anna and I freaked out. I wasn't sure what to do. My first instinct was to make sure Tina was safe. In all honesty, I tried telling you while you were suspending me, but ..."

"You did? I'm so sorry. I was just so mad. I guess I wasn't hearing what you were trying to tell me. I apologize," Randy said.

"No need to apologize. I'm just appreciative you gave me my job back."

The server came over and took their drink and appetizer orders—truffle fries and mozzarella sticks for the table, strawberry margaritas for Kelsey and Joanna, and beer for Randy and Josh. Both Tina and Brian decided on fresh strawberry lemonades.

"We all need to be vigilant about being aware of our surroundings. We don't know who sent Josh and Kelsey the messages or if it's even the same person. And we don't know if it's the killer. It may be someone who knows something about Anna's killer. You haven't received any messages, Tina?" Randy said.

Tina replied, "No, not at all. That is odd when you think about it."

Chapter 81

"Thank you for meeting me. This means a lot," Josh said as he shook Leo's hand. Kelsey and Tina quietly sat down, observing the interaction.

Leo had a tear in his eye as he took Josh's hand in both of his. "I helped deliver you, you know? Me and Anna. Wow, I can't believe you're an adult."

Josh smiled and said, "It's certainly been a while."

"Hi, Uncle Leo," Tina said, standing and hugging him. Leo gave her a big squeeze and a kiss on the top of her head.

"Hello, Kelsey. Nice to see you, too. So, what do I have the pleasure of helping you all with this evening?" Leo said as he took a seat. The waitress brought over glasses of ice water and placed their menus down.

"I wanted to ask you something—something I'm confused about," Josh said. "I called my parents this morning, and they told me that the money in my trust fund came from you even though it was being transferred over from Anna's bank account. Because it was an open adoption, no one felt this was strange.

My parents were grateful for the account and it made them feel secure that I had a good nest egg if something had happened to them when I was a kid. But all this time we thought Anna was my mother."

Leo sighed and then grumbled something inaudibly.

"What are you not telling us, Uncle Leo?" Tina said. "Spill it."

If there was one person who could talk to Leo like this, it was Tina. Just as he had loved Anna with all his heart, Tina was the apple of his eye. He was there for all her milestones and treated her more like a daughter than a niece. Anna and Nick had asked him to be Tina's godfather before she was born.

Leo looked up, his fists bunched up in frustration. "Okay, okay. I promised I wouldn't ever tell anyone. I guess it doesn't really matter now, though. Sven. My father. He wanted to make sure you were taken care of. His affair with Anna's mother was brief, and he didn't want another kid. He hid it from everyone but me. I was his gopher. He had me take money out of his bank account, deposit it into mine, and then transfer it to Anna for your trust every month. He didn't want the paper trail to be traced back to him. He wouldn't even let me tell Anna he was the father. She thought the money came from me. To help out, you know?"

Josh looked at him, even more confused. He looked at Tina, and she shrugged.

"Why didn't he want anyone to know?" Josh asked.

"The old man is crazy. At first, it was because he didn't want my mother to find out. He didn't want her to leave him and take his money with her. But then, after my mom passed away,

I think he was just ashamed and didn't want anyone to know what a coward he was for not fessing up to having another kid."

"We're having a hard time connecting any of this to my mom's death," Tina said. "Do you think this is related?"

"Tina and I stand to inherit most of Anna's estate except her company which will be dissolved and split into three disbursements. The beneficiaries are you, Nick, and Tina. All of us have alibis, so unless one of us hired someone to kill Anna, what kind of motive would the killer have to kill her?" Josh added.

"Yes, that's correct. But that's looking at it from a perspective that someone wanted to kill her and that it wasn't an accident by a random burglar," Leo said.

"Uncle, how can you still think this was an accident? Look at the messages Josh and Kelsey have received. These are deliberate threats. Probably from the killer," Tina said as Kelsey and Josh showed Leo the messages they had received.

Leo took a minute to process the information. He looked stunned.

"I had no idea. I know you asked Jason and me if we sent you a text to stay away or something of that matter, but who would send these? Have you noticed anyone following you?" Leo asked.

"No, but I work with the public, so I see a lot of people every day. But I'm always aware of my surroundings. There hasn't been anyone suspicious," Kelsey said.

"Same here. Nothing out of the ordinary," Josh added.

"Tina, I think we need to sit down and discuss this with your aunt since she's an attorney and can probably look at this from another point of view. I'd like your dad to join us, too. I don't like how we three have the biggest motives. I would never do anything to hurt your mom. Never.

But we need to get down to the bottom of this," Leo said. "Your Auntie Mae will figure it out. She's a sharp one."

Chapter 82

Tuesday, October 11, 2022

M ae sat scrolling through her phone and sipped her Americano while waiting for Leo, Nick, and Tina to arrive. The trio walked in a few minutes later sitting down, one by one at Mae's table.

"Okay, I'm here. Speak." Mae said, getting straight to business.

"We didn't kill Anna, Mae. You know this." Nick said.

"Well, of course you didn't. But who did? If it wasn't you three? Josh didn't even know he was in the will," Mae said.

"What about Abby, David, and Jason? Maybe one of them was mad at Anna about something," Leo said.

"I think David had a little *thing* for Anna if you ask me. I don't know if Abby caught on to that, but even if she had, she wouldn't have said a bad word about Anna. That's just how our sister is," Mae said.

"What would one of them be mad at her for? And mad enough to kill her? Why would they try to hide me if it was one of them? That doesn't make sense," Tina said. "Plus, I was with Jason that night."

"You're right. You're right," Leo said. "Who else would benefit from Anna dying and Kelsey and Josh staying out of the picture?"

"Didn't you say Kelsey was trying to help solve Anna's murder? Maybe the killer just wanted her out of the way. And Josh is a police officer. He is not only inheriting something from the estate, but he has a personal motive to find out who Anna's killer is. They're in the way of the killer getting whatever they want," Mae said.

"That makes sense," Nick said.

"I received the adoption papers from the agency and Josh's birth certificate. We will do a formal reading of the will this Friday at seven p.m. at the house." Mae turned to Tina. "Also, we will have the memorial for your mother this Saturday. Her ashes are at the funeral home waiting for you, dear. I didn't want to rush you though. The memorial will be at Grandmother and Pop Pop's house at one." Mae looked at her watch and said, "Oh, look at the time. I should get back to the courthouse. I will see you all on Friday."

She stood up to leave, digging around in her purse for her keys with one hand, her phone in the other. "Dammit, where are they?"

"Honey," Leo said as he tossed her the keys to her Porsche. Reaching to catch them, her diamond wedding ring sparkled as it caught the light. Blowing him a kiss, she then dialed her assistant and was off.

"Did Mae end up getting interviewed by the police?" Nick asked Leo.

"She thought it was unnecessary to be interviewed because she had an alibi," Leo said.

"She was with a client working late. The client gave the police a statement."

"Isn't that a conflict of interest?" Nick said, "Because she's working for the client?"

"There's camera footage of her entering the courthouse library and not leaving until nine p.m.," Leo said, shrugging. "Why? Are you suspicious of your own sister?"

"Tina, honey what's wrong," Nick said, reaching for her. Tina's face looked as if she had just seen a ghost.

"I've got to go. Kelsey's waiting for me in the truck," Tina said as she got up and rushed out.

Passing two police officers on her way out, Tina turned as she heard, "Leo Eriksen, you have the right to remain silent."

"Nick! I didn't do it! I promise!" Leo shouted. "Tina, have Kelsey call her dad. I have proof. Tell him I can prove it. I was at the bank."

The officers handcuffed Leo and led him out to the police car as Tina climbed up into Chuckie. "I know who killed my mom," she said to Kelsey, her face white as a ghost, "and it wasn't my Uncle Leo."

Chapter 83

Tuesday, October 11, 2022

"Dad, Leo didn't do it. We know who did," Kelsey yelled into her phone as she and Tina raced to the police station.

"Kelsey! What? We found the murder weapon. It was wrapped in one of Leo's shirts."

"But he had an alibi. There's no way he could be in two places at once. Where was the weapon found?"

"Buried in Oakview Park. Someone's dog dug it up. It was a metal wine holder covered in dried blood. Anna's blood," Randy said as he frantically looked through the case file.

"Dad, the killer is Mae," Kelsey said. "We're at the front door. Can you come let us in?"

Randy rushed to the front door of the station and hustled them in. "Here, let's go to my office," he said. "Keep your voices low so no one else hears."

"We just have to prove it," Kelsey said.

Randy sat down. "Tell me what you know."

"So, you know how the killer was lefthanded? When my uncle tossed my aunt her keys at the café today, she caught them perfectly in her left hand," Tina said. "On our drive here, Kelsey and I realized that even though Mae isn't a beneficiary of the will, she will inherit money because Leo will take one-third of the company. She benefits from my mom's death."

"Plus, if Leo is indicted for murder, she gets all of it," Kelsey added. "That's probably why she wrapped the weapon in his shirt. It wasn't an accident. She was trying to frame him. She was mad because she thought he had a child with Anna. Also, doesn't Nick inherit part of the company as well? His portion of the company would wipe out his gambling debts. Mae felt Anna wronged Nick by cheating on him. She was just as angry as Nick when she discovered Tina wasn't his. This was her revenge on Anna. Taking care of herself, and her brother."

"That's right! She was probably even madder than my dad," Tina added.

"Mae," Randy said, nodding. "This makes sense, girls, but we need solid evidence. Leo's shirt wrapped around the murder weapon is pretty solid. We'll subpoena the footage from the bank, but I don't know how much it will help."

"We need to go back to the scene of the crime," Kelsey said. "Someone saw something."

Chapter 84

Wednesday, October 12, 2022

Anticipation churned in Kelsey's stomach as she thought about the task ahead. She had canceled her afternoon training sessions, and she, Justin, and Tina were preparing to scour Anna's neighborhood for evidence. Despite Detective Hart's thorough sweeps of the area surrounding the crime scene, a few residents hadn't been home during the searches. Earlier in the day, Tina had texted Kelsey the list of houses Randy had given them, detailing the addresses of the neighbors who couldn't be reached. There were only twelve houses on Tina's end of the cul-de-sac and twelve on the other side, so Hart only talked to twenty of the houses on the entire block. With the information in hand, Kelsey felt both determined and nervous as she texted back, *hoping the four missing people are home today. fingers crossed.*

Five o'clock rolled around, and Justin and Kelsey picked up Tina.

"Okay, so I've got three copies of the spreadsheet I made. Here are clipboards and pens, too. We have a lot of houses to cover. The spreadsheet has the address and police notes, if any. I also did an owner's search on each house and wrote the missing names in. We should start with the people Hart didn't contact," Tina said.

"Nice job. Now breathe. Holy moly, you are like that squirrel from that one movie who drinks a bunch of coffee, and no one can understand him," Kelsey said.

"Oh, I love that movie! *Hoodwinked*!" Justin said, holding out his bag of Haribo gummy bears to Kelsey and Tina.

"Yeah, that's it! Okay, so Tina your plan sounds perfect. I say—for safety reasons—we stick together instead of splitting up," Kelsey said, taking a small handful of bears, picking the red ones out, and putting the rest of them back in Justin's bag.

"Hey!" he said, and Tina giggled.

"The reds are my favorite too!" Tina said, as she gave Kelsey a high five.

The trio set off, each armed with a spreadsheet, clipboard, and pen.

First up was Julie Appleby's house. Hart interviewed her, but his notes needed clarification. His chicken scratch was illegible. Julie was Tina's next-door neighbor, and she and Anna loved trading baked goods on the weekend.

"Hi, Mrs. Appleby. It's Tina."

"Oh, hello, dear. Are you back home from college? How is your mom?"

Mrs. Appleby was confused.

"Oh, yes, I'm home for now. Is Julie home?"

"Oh, yes, she is. Let me call her. Here, come in you three, and have a cup of tea with a little old lady. Julie!" she called up the stairs.

A young woman in her mid-thirties came down. When she saw Tina, she said, "Oh, Tina. I'm so sorry I haven't been in touch. I'm so sorry to hear about your mom."

"Hi, Julie. Actually, that's why we're here. This is my sister Kelsey and our friend Justin. We're asking people on the block if they saw or heard anything the night my mom was killed. I know the police have already spoken to you, but since you live next door, I wanted to double-check to see if you remembered anything."

"Unfortunately, we didn't see or hear anything that night. My mom was asleep already, and I was out at a work dinner downtown."

"What time did you get back home?" Tina asked.

"Well, it had to be about ten o'clock or so. The police and first responders were at your house when I got home. When I entered our house, my mom was still sound asleep in bed. I asked her the following morning if she had heard anything, and she said she hadn't. Of course, her hearing isn't the best these days. I wish I could help. Are you asking the other neighbors as well?"

"Yes, we're working our way around the block."

"Oh, good. Maybe ask the guy who lives across the street from you. He doesn't seem to be home a lot, but who knows if he has one of those doorbell cameras or something?"

"That's a good idea, Julie. Thank you so much for your time, and thank you, Mrs. Appleby!"

"Oh, goodbye, dear. Say hello to your mother for me," Mrs. Appleby said.

"I think it's a good idea for us to check the guy across the street for a camera," Kelsey said, looking at the spreadsheet. "The person in that house was never home when Hart did his searches."

Justin rang the doorbell, and a man answered. He was wearing a blue button-down shirt, tan Dockers, and brown leather dress shoes.

"Oh, hey, guys. I'm sorry. I was expecting someone else. Are you selling something?" he said, eyeing the clipboards.

"Oh, we're sorry to bother you. No, we're not selling anything. My mom and I lived in that house over there." Tina pointed out.

"Oh, yeah. I think I met your mom the week I moved here. It was about three years ago, and she brought me a welcome basket. Nice lady in her mid-forties, about yay high, long brown hair?"

"Yep. That's my mom. She does that for all the all the new neighbors. I mean, she did that."

Kelsey could see Tina start to break down while talking about her mom, so she took over the conversation. "Umm, so anyways, I'm Kelsey and this is Tina and he's Justin. And Anna, Tina's mom, was murdered last month."

His eyes opened wide in shock. "Oh, I'm so sorry. Here, come in. How rude of me not to let my own neighbor in."

Kelsey, Justin, and Tina entered the barely furnished home. There was a desk with a huge computer set up on it, an armchair, and a TV. Kelsey noticed that the computer setup was a lot like Sam's.

As if reading her mind, he said, "I know, I know, total bachelor pad. I'm never home, so even though my stuff's been here for three years, I've probably only been living here for three or four months in total. I travel for work."

"What do you do, if you don't mind me asking?" Tina said.

"I'm a celebrity private investigator. Name's Rick Shields."

"It's nice to meet you, Rick," Justin said.

"So, we should probably say why we're knocking on your door," Kelsey continued. "We think we know who killed Anna, but we don't have any solid proof. We were hoping you have a doorbell camera that might help us. I know it's a big ask, but—"

"That's not a big ask at all. I'm a PI. I have camera surveillance that runs twenty-four seven," Rick said, smiling.

Chapter 85

R ick walked the trio over to his large desktop set-up—three monitors and a huge hard drive tower that made whirring noises. He touched the mouse, and all three screens came to life. After clicking a few buttons, the neighborhood appeared on the middle and right screens.

"Okay, so there are eight cameras in total. As you can see, there aren't any blind spots, and the cameras are pretty clear."

Tina took a deep breath and said, "Can we see the footage from the night my mom was killed?"

Rick typed in the date and time they were looking for and hit play. One of his cameras was angled directly at Anna's house. Rick sped up the footage to double time, and at six p.m., they saw a dark sedan pull into the house's driveway.

"That's my dad's car," Tina said.

They observed Nick ringing the doorbell. Anna answered, and Nick pushed his way in, closing the door behind him. About ten minutes later, Nick left, and Anna was in the doorway shouting something after him. She was touching her face.

"All of this coincides with what your dad told us. Your mom was still alive when he left. We can see her right there," Justin said, pointing to Anna on the screen.

"You guys want a snack? I think I have a bag of chips somewhere here. Here's some bottled water while you're working," Rick said as he handed each of them a bottle.

"Oh, no, I think we're good. Thanks though. You're helping us plenty by letting us see this footage. Your cameras have such good resolution. I could see my dad's expression when he left the house and everything," Tina said to Rick.

"Yeah, these are top-of-the-line," Rick said, sitting down in the armchair. They continued to watch the footage and arrived at the part where Tina found her mom. Tina put her hands over her mouth and gasped.

"Wait, no one came or left between when your dad left and you arrived," Kelsey said, "Rewind to the part where your dad left, and let's watch it in real time."

They watched the video for a few minutes, and at about 7:32, Kelsey said, "Stop! Did you see that?"

They rewound the video, and Tina scrubbed it to run in slow motion. They saw the front door open a little and then close.

"I saw that!" Justin said, pointing to the screen.

Rick got up from where he was sitting and watched the footage replay. "Whoever it was must have come and gone through the back. Maybe the person thought they could leave out the front and then thought better of it," he said. "Sorry to not be more help."

"No, no, this was so helpful. Okay, so at seven thirty-two, the killer had already killed my mom and was leaving. At least we know that now."

"Those houses back up to the park, right?" Rick asked.

"Yeah, our yard is open with no back fence and goes directly into the grassy park area. Why?"

"And beyond the grassy park area is a group of apartment buildings, right?" he continued.

"Exactly."

"Have you asked anyone in the apartment complex if they saw anything?"

"We didn't even think of that," Kelsey said.

"I have nothing better to do tonight. The person who was going to come over just canceled on me. Can I tag along?" Rick said, grabbing his binoculars.

"That would be awesome," Tina said, perking up. "We could use a PI right about now. Everything so far has been a dead end."

They left Rick's house and walked to the apartment complex behind Tina's house. When they arrived at the grassy area, Rick said, "Wait." Looking up at the building through binoculars, he pointed and said, "There. We need to see who lives in that apartment."

They saw a large telescope in the window of one of the apartments.

After knocking on the door of the building manager, a tall, blonde woman in her mid-fifties answered.

"Hi, can I help you?" she said.

"Hi, we're hoping you can," Kelsey said. She introduced herself, Tina, Justin, and Rick to the woman and told her their objective.

"I know exactly who you're talking about. The telescope belongs to a scientist who works at SETI. Have you heard of it?"

"Yes, actually, I have," Kelsey said. "My client Janet works there."

"He loves looking at the stars and constellations and all that stuff. He brags about that telescope. It's a very high-powered one and very expensive. Here, let's go see if he's home. I'm Marcia, by the way." They followed Marcia to the apartment, and a man in his early sixties opened the door. Marcia explained the situation.

"I'm Professor Whitley. You can call me Bob, though," he said. "My telescope is usually pointed at the stars, but that night, there was a lot of commotion at the house you're talking about. It caught my attention."

They followed him into his relatively spacious bedroom where his telescope was. He waved Rick over and said, "Look here. You can see what kind of view I have. I'll point it toward the sky so you can see what I mean."

Rick peeked into the telescope and said, "Wow, that really is amazing. I can see planets."

They took turns looking into the telescope and complimenting Bob on the fine piece of equipment.

"So, if that's what you can see in the sky, what can you see on the ground?" Kelsey asked.

"Here, take a look yourself," Bob said, pointing the telescope down to Tina's house.

"It's like you're standing in the backyard!" Tina said.

"So, what kind of commotion did you see that night?" Justin asked.

"Well, I didn't know what I was seeing at the time. To any lay person, it would just be someone going in and out of the house, but it was odd because the grass was very wet that night, and the woman was wearing heels. She looked panicked and in a hurry. Of course, I didn't want to appear like a peeping Tom, so I just kept the photos to myself. I had no idea someone was murdered that night. I don't watch the news very much. Very depressing."

"Did you say photos?" Rick said, and Bob walked over to his bedroom dresser and opened the top drawer. From it, he withdrew some printed photographs.

"I don't usually take photos of what I'm looking at, but that lady. She was something. She was waving her arms like she was frantic and paced back and forth on the lawn before leaving. I guess I just thought it was strange," Bob said, handing Kelsey the photos.

"Oh my god. That's Mae!" Kelsey gasped. "The photo's time stamp is at seven thirty-four p.m. We need to get these to the police."

"Thank you so much," Tina said, giving Bob a big hug. "Thank you, thank you, thank you! You just proved who killed my mom. I owe you everything."

"Oh, dear. You're welcome. I'm just sorry I didn't come forward with the photographs sooner. Had I of known..."

"No, no, you did great."

They left the apartment, thanking Marcia for her help.

"Well, I guess this is it," Rick said. "Case solved."

"Thank you so much, Rick. For everything." Tina said.

"Well, if you ever need a PI, you know where to go. Oh, and take this." He reached into his back pocket and took his wallet out. He pulled a business card out of it and handed it to Tina.

"My cell number is on there in case you ever need me."

Chapter 86

Wednesday, October 12, 2022

"Dad, can you meet us at the station? We have proof Mae killed Anna."

"What? Kels, are you kidding me? I'm on my way," Randy replied.

Within two minutes, Randy's car screeched into the station's lot. Unlocking the front door, he hustled them into his office.

"Okay, so what is this evidence you have?" he said, a little out of breath.

"Here. You can see for yourself," Tina said, handing him the envelope of photographs.

Randy carefully took them out and looked.

"Well, I'll be damned. It really is Mae. The resolution on this camera is amazing."

After Randy made a call, he turned to his daughters and their friend, and said, "They're on their way to get Mae right now. We've got Leo in custody, but it looks like we'll be releasing him soon."

"I have a question, Dad. Didn't you get the bank footage that showed Leo at the ATM?" Kelsey asked.

"We did. The time stamp on the ATM footage was seven twenty-two p.m. So, according to these photos, the murder must have happened right after he visited the bank. It happened within minutes. Since the police only had a timeframe for Anna's death and not the exact time of the crime, this didn't necessarily clear him. But it also didn't mean he did it. His shirt was circumstantial, and Mae would have easily had access to his clothing without him even knowing. Whether or not he knew is a different story."

Chapter 87

Thursday, October 13, 2022

Detective Hart—Interview with Mae Scott Eriksen

Detective Hart: Recording. Date: Thursday, October 20, 2022. 1:25 p.m. I am interviewing Mae Scott Eriksen with her Attorney, Sigmund Larimore, present. Mae Eriksen, do you swear to tell the truth?

Mae: I do.

Detective Hart: Please tell us what happened on the evening of Tuesday, September 13.

Mae: I wanted to talk to Anna about the money Leo was giving her. I didn't feel it was fair for him to be giving her money when he said the kid wasn't even his. Secretly, I thought it was his, though. Why would he be stupid and give money to a kid if it wasn't?

Detective Hart: What do you do for a living, Mrs. Eriksen?

Mae: I'm a very well-known high-powered attorney in the area, Detective. I'm sure you've seen my advertisements everywhere.

Detective Hart: As a high-powered attorney, I would think you would make plenty of money for your household. Why be bothered by your husband giving Anna money? You don't have children, do you?

Mae: That's not the point!

Detective Hart: Okay, let's get back to that night. You were angry Leo was giving Anna money.

You wanted to talk to Anna about it. Is that correct?

Mae: Yes.

Detective Hart: So, then what happened?

Mae: Anna and I started arguing. She told me I didn't know what I was talking about. I told her she was taking money from my family. Leo had funded her successful business, *and* he was giving her money. She was a greedy little bitch. She hid money from Nick while they were married. No wonder he had gambling debt. Anyway, while we were arguing, I realized that things would be easier for everyone if Anna was out of the picture.

Detective Hart: Better for whom?

Mae: Everyone! Leo, me, Nick, Tina. Her company is worth millions. She owed our family for her successful business. My brother *and* husband both helped her. And how did she show her gratitude? I'll tell you. She didn't.

Detective Hart: Okay, so during the altercation, you killed Anna?

Attorney Sigmund Larimore: My client doesn't have to answer that.

Detective Hart: Why was your husband's shirt wrapped around the murder weapon?

Mae: Why don't you ask him?

Detective Hart: Mrs. Eriksen, did you kill Anna Scott?

Mae: No comment.

[End of interview]

Chapter 88

The past few weeks had been an exhilarating whirlwind of adventure and discovery. Fox Fitness was positively buzzing with energy, and both Kelsey and Justin were back to their long days of dynamic training sessions, pushing their clients to new heights.

Kelsey and Josh were still in the delightful early stages of getting to know one another. Josh was thrilled to have a newfound family and eagerly planned for Kelsey to join him in Seattle that winter to visit his parents and sister. Things were moving fast.

The best part was that Tina could finally start living her life without fear. She had returned to work part time and was studying to become an attorney. Tina now lived permanently with Saffron, and they, along with Kelsey and Charlie, had established a monthly girls' night tradition. Tina also enjoyed attending the James' family brunches where Brian loved having another sister and Joanna and Randy treated her like she had always been a part of the family.

While Kelsey and Justin still hung out, it had become less frequent since Kelsey started seeing Josh. Justin and Audrey were taking their relationship slow, with Audrey frequently seeking Kelsey's advice on Justin's likes and dislikes. Kelsey loved the way Justin snuck glances at Audrey during her training sessions. The banter between Kelsey and Justin continued; she still playfully punched him in the arm on shoulder day, and he still affectionately called her "Kelsey Sue."

Mae, facing legal battles, managed to plead down to second-degree murder and was sentenced to thirty years in state prison. Leo liked not being nagged to pick his dirty socks off the floor. Temporarily, at least. With good behavior, Mae would be out in ten years.

As for Finley, the adorable gym mascot, he was as happy as ever, delighting everyone at Fox Fitness with his daily quest for treats and attention.